Sunita's Short Stories

Sunita Tohan

ISBN: 979-8-9938482-0-4

I dedicate this book to all the people who believed I was enough. The ones who supported my journey and accepted me for who I am. I am forever indebted - from the heart of Sunita

My two pillars: Sanjay & Sunil

Contents

Prologue...1

Part I: Gratitude in the Everyday 2

Part II: Lessons from the Past...38

Part III: Beauty Is in Acceptance..75

Part IV: Moving Forward 117

Part V: The Ordinary that Shapes 157

Prologue

If a writer falls for you, you'll never die...

You will live on through the words that are woven. The beauty of knowing someone special is that missing them means they live on in the mind and heart. Every memory will be relived through unspoken words. The blank pages will eventually fill with the moments when time stood still. They will reflect the emotions that were felt.

And so, as I write, I weave a tapestry of the time we spent together. It won't matter whether we belonged or the length of our togetherness. These blank pages will flow with lyrics and scripts of our union. You and I, and the picture we illustrated, will be threaded in a journal bound with deep affection and interlaced with devotion.

Some emotions are simply felt. They cannot be explained, and then some emotions erupt, and can be beautifully expressed as sentiments that bridge the heart. Tomorrow was never promised, so today I word each chapter. I know the depth to which my words seek validation, and this mind can bring to life scenarios that can move your universe, sink the heart, and shed a tear.

You'll live on in my world and in the world of those who interpret these scriptures. They will know exactly how heavenly the space between us felt and how this masterpiece came together, one word at a time. It will matter little how much time passed, but years from now, when you do happen to stumble upon this story, know that you never died, because this writer kept you alive one word at a time...

PART I

Gratitude in the Everyday

Gratitude isn't only for grand moments - it's in the warmth of tea, the hush of the morning, and the unexpected hug.

- Practice Gratitude Page 3
- Today's Horoscope Page 5
- Friends and Coffee Page 7
- Trust the Process Page 10
- Good Morning Page 13
- I Miss You Page 15
- Thank You! Page 17
- Sharing is Caring Page 20
- Take a Break Page 23
- Floating Page 25
- The Walk Page 26
- Sent with Love Page 28
- Time Will Tell Page 30
- Giving Away a Son Page 33
- Going Home Page 35

Practice Gratitude

At times, it takes one small experience to learn a big lesson. It doesn't have to be a mistake per se, but at times, we need to absorb reality before we grasp a point. I have had an eventful life, managed ups and downs, and digested difficult stages. I welcomed happy moments and sustained a life worth living. Some phases of my life came down on me like a landslide. I've spent days feeling sorry for myself, bitter and exhausted. Other times, I've been more than pleased, happy with an outcome.

It wasn't until I landed a voluntary position writing children's stories that I encountered appreciation differently. I learned the power of giving and the meaning of being blessed. The children I interview are from the third world, impoverished, from marginal communities, and less developed regions.

They live lives that don't even compare to mine. I felt ashamed that I complained about things that they don't even know exist. They live on the bare minimum; at times, they barely live. The problems they face are on a different spectrum, and mine seem minuscule in comparison. I lose my appetite because too much nonsense fills my brain, and these children don't even know what an appetite is. I have a roof over my head; I choose clothes every day, and I drink water without even thinking. I felt ashamed and nauseous at the thought that I criticize, mock, and judge. I feel embarrassed to think I complain at all.

I teach, and some of my students need mentoring. Lending them an ear or simply engaging in conversation helps them in ways I can't explain. It's an assurance of a kind that someone out there in the world is listening and understands. It's this guidance and support that becomes a priceless commodity. Someone believes they can do better. Perhaps I give them my time because it was the one thing that I didn't receive: to be heard. Because to be acknowledged and accepted is an important part of one's life.

When I began this journey of giving, it led me to believe that I wasn't just helping; I was making a difference. The more I committed, the more satisfying it became. Giving my time, my knowledge, and my support provided me with a sense of purpose. I wasn't just helping them; they were helping me. These children taught me the true meaning of gratitude and how to stay grounded. How something so simple can make a big impact. To make their life a little better today, all I have to do is welcome them. It's that simple. Merely interacting with some positivity and kindness makes their day. I make them feel appreciated and heard.

I'm able to value my own life because of this journey. I recognized my achievements, and I cherished the blessings. Little things don't bother me as much anymore. I'm learning to accept how grateful I am for all that I have. I can utilize my talents for the betterment of others, and I am honored to assist and do my part to touch the lives of a few.

Our first-world problems are mere frustrations. We have become so accustomed to a life of comfort and convenience that we don't think twice, nor do we appreciate it. We all have the basics to survive. Yet practicing gratitude for the wealth we have obtained or simply for life itself is neglected and becomes unworthy.

Today's Horoscope

I reach for my phone to check my horoscope. I do it almost every morning; it's a kind of ritual. I think checking it makes me believe the planets will do some magic, and my world will be different.

The truth is, the planets do shift, and I do believe they affect us. Ironically, most days they are right about my intentions, feelings, and mood. I'm a thinker, so they relate to my thoughts, and it makes me feel like I'm being heard. If the stars align, they create a favorable outcome, and it elevates my mood. Funny, isn't it? They're just words, yet the magnitude of the effect they have on me is somewhat surprising. Deep down, I believe we all live with some kind of insecurity, some imbalance, and trauma. I think everyone also yearns for positivity, to be accepted and encouraged.

Someone asked me if I really believe in horoscopes. I thought a lot today about why reading the horoscope meant anything to me at all. People around the world, born on the same planet in the same era, do hold some small connection to the stars. I concluded that I need to read those words of wisdom, positivity, and clarity, because I feel the need to rise above and ascend, and have some hope and determination, and if, for this transformation, I need to read some scripts, then my horoscope is investing in my happiness.

Everyone needs to know that they are being heard. Being alone means I don't have that person beside me to guide me, to believe in me, and to tell me it's going to be okay. I'm missing that individual beside me who shares my emotions and lifts me. So, each morning when I reach out for my horoscope, I'm reaching for some positive words of comfort and encouragement to start my day, and it's as if I'm reaching for that missing person.

Friends and Coffee

I scan the menu as if it's the first time I've sat at this coffee shop. I already know my preference, and yet I feel the need to browse just in case I missed something on the menu the last time I was here. I laugh out loud with my friend as I humor her. We meet frequently and embark on conversations over coffee. I enjoy her company; we have a lot in common. Suddenly, I feel my phone vibrate in my bag, and I fumble around for it. It's my best friend calling, and I want to answer because it's an odd time for her to call. We have our scheduled time, as distance has become a hurdle, and so she takes precedence.

I ponder friendships. The word "friend" doesn't need a prefix; it says a lot just on its own. A good friend should be there for you, to be able to laugh with you, lend a shoulder, and be loyal. Simple traits, nothing fancy. But with the title comes expectations, and those expectations cannot be met throughout one lifetime. People come in and out of your life; some drift, and some remain. Some take away a part of you, and some leave you with lessons. Friends cross your path for a reason. Sometimes we grow apart from each other, and we no longer find things in common. Life happens, and then distance pulls you away; we evolve. That is how the world turns, how we progress.

In my life, I've been hurt by friends, I've consoled them, and I have shared some of the happiest moments with them. I have old friends who have seen me through most of my life, others just my adult life, and some that I've only known for a year or two. I have friends who don't know much about me, and a few who have lived my story. Some I don't see for years at a time, and others hold a bond that makes life unimaginable without them. How do some friends become such a big part of your life? These strangers from different worlds become your family; it is true, they become the family that you choose. Family members are permanent, and you have to learn to get along. These "family" friends you handpick.

Close friends hold secrets about each other that only they will take to the grave. They are with you through the ups and downs that life throws your way. Anyone will celebrate in your joys, but only a select few will walk with you in your time of sorrow. Those are your true friends, the ones that won't let the second tear shed. The ones that know how to make you smile and the ones that will scold you, criticize you, and run to you when no one is around for comfort. I consider you blessed if you have even one of these; they are the antidote to this chaotic, inconsistent life. You need them to safeguard.

We make friends in every stage of our life, and in each stage we look for qualities that will suffice our needs then. But there are those few souls with whom we maintain a strong link in all those stages because they shed love of another kind, one that looks past your imperfections. They adhere to your heart and tie a bond that joins deep emotions. They enhance your well-being. You hold a mutual connection, and your traits match; you hold each other up without fear of judgment.

No one is perfect. You take a friend with their good qualities and the bad ones, then you weigh them. We all do it unconsciously. When the good qualities outweigh the bad ones AND you can look past them, then you can rest assured you made a good choice. Good friendship also means you are willing to stand up for each other's beliefs; you can forgive and are willing to walk that extra mile, and you need to love without conditions. Each friend in your life holds a different position on the ladder. Just like no person is alike, each friendship is not the same. You cannot replace a person or friendship, and no other can fill that space. Complicated relationships don't work. Friendship shouldn't be work. It shouldn't be a daunting task; it should flow, effortlessly, simply.

I take a sip of my tepid coffee and smile. My friend is surprised I'm okay with drinking it now that it's lost its zest. Oh, but I'd forsake my favorite cup of java anytime to listen to a friend in need. Friendship is a lot like coffee. They come from different parts of the world, and no bean is identical; no roast is similar in taste. Every sip should make you feel worthy; every cup should leave you feeling mellow and warm. If it's too bitter, you add a bit of sweetness to offset it, and if it's not meant to be, you let it go. You can always revisit it again, and if not, you can always try tea.

Trust the Process

The candle flickers, and I grab my teacup. I'm too lazy this evening to switch on the lamp, and so my scented candle brings on an illusion of ease. I sink into the cushions, hoping I don't have to move for some time. I feel insanely proud that I have everything I need at arm's length. My favorite tunes play in the background, and my remotes are on standby. It's unlikely I'll finish my book this evening, but another one sits beneath it, you know, just in case a miracle were to happen.

I grab my laptop and go over my calendar. It's then that I realize that just a few weeks ago, I was prancing around on a mini vacay, and in one split second, everything changed. I now sit here with my fractured foot propped up on a cushion. There was no warning, no alert, just a sudden fall, and everything changed in a split second.

The first week, I spent cursing myself at my own stupidity. I was immobilized, in pain, and very frustrated. For the next two weeks, I eventually succumbed to the disability, a bit like the piece of chocolate that is now melting between my fingers. This mishap taught me a few lessons, perhaps I needed to re-learn. I realized I needed to be more aware. Composure is essential; how else do we control ourselves? In most stages of my life, I was never in a temperate state, but today I have become more placid than ever before. I accepted the defeat, and I learned how to tackle it with an equable state rather than fight it with agitation. Worrying over my negligence wouldn't help it heal faster. This too shall pass, I told myself, and in no time, I'll be on my feet again.

Time passes by; it should pass unruffled. When the hurdles appear, we should deal with them with an open mind rather than avoid them. It's beneficial for you to do a little spring cleaning of your mind from time to time. If scenarios or people aren't operating on your frequency, it's time to let them go. We unknowingly become accommodating to clutter. A year ago, I was still inviting it, but today I diplomatically bypassed the first sight of foreseen turmoil.

We live in a constant state of anxiety on different levels; most of the time, it's an underlying pulsation, but very much alive. Our subconscious is accustomed to instant results. Having composure takes effort. I find that when I am still and calm, that is when the most positivity is acquired. It is then that I focus and become the most phlegmatic. Everyone should master stillness, but we resist a passive state. We are quick-tempered in such a way that our wants and needs become priorities over self-assurance, level-headedness, and above all, patience.

In my respite, I voluntarily surrendered to my disability and slowly began to ease my nerves. My days were spent mostly occupying my mind with uncomplicated, effortless tasks. The more I relaxed, the more my stiffness released, and the more of what didn't matter so much, I let go. We tend to tense up with all the uncertain outcomes. It took me a long time to learn to embrace the moments. Nothing much was going to change if I stole some minutes from the busyness. We need to be reminded of the journey, that it's not always a race. We need to acquire stillness and maneuver at our own pace, so that we can soak up and surrender to the moments. Life is passing by no matter what happens, so why rush it when time can walk beside you?

As I continue scanning through my year, it dawns on me that so much has changed in not just one week but even this year, too. Two seasons passed, seven months came to an end, birthdays came and went. I am not the same person I was a year ago. We are constantly evolving. Stumbling on accidents teaches us lessons. How else do we reinvent ourselves? It mostly happens when things go wrong. You have to make mistakes to realize what didn't work. Our style changes with the decades that pass, and so the same applies to the process in which we find ourselves. Why settle for basics when you can flourish and dance off the beaten path? Transformation is a wonderful thing.

Give yourself a chance. Give yourself time. Life happens just like that; we move on, and so much changes without us even knowing. It's important to become aware. My calendar has a few months left this year. Rather than fill them up with an agenda, I've chosen to leave them blank. When tomorrow comes, I'll embrace it and every day after, each day as it comes, one day at a time. Trusting the process.

Good Morning

As a human having resided on this planet for quite some time, I have become a witness to the race as a whole. Having also had the privilege to experience people from all walks of life, I am still surprised by the actions and behaviors some humans portray. On my daily walks, I meet people, some regular walkers like me, some strangers, and I always smile and wish a good morning to everyone.

There are a select few who choose to ignore me or fail to make eye contact; some of these few I see every day, and it began to bother me. I would conjure up thoughts about my appearance or that perhaps they were having a bad morning, and I didn't deserve a response back. But does repeated ignorance deserve a second thought?

It took me a long time to understand that regulating my thoughts plays a huge role in my reaction to someone's behavior. It took even longer for me to come to terms with the fact that I cannot change another person, and similarly, another person's actions shouldn't move me either.

Negativity no doubt brings you down; it also affects those who surround you. Negativity and toxic auras are created because of some underlying damaging experiences that slowly begin to surface in other ways and are hard to tackle and even harder to shake off. Jealousy, anger, and other such traits begin to erupt. You lash out because it makes you feel better in the moment, but in reality, you need to look inward at what it is that is disturbing you and get to the root cause.

Someone's bad behavior and insults really have nothing to do with me; it's something personal within themselves that only they can fix. The bigger problem here is that a sensitive, vulnerable person will no doubt take this behavior personally, when in reality it has nothing to do with them.

Coming to terms with one's flaws and seeking avenues to heal are important to begin to break the barrier. Yet it is the hardest thing to do. A cycle of unfortunate, unconstructive, and damaging habits develop that are hard to break, and before long, you become a negative, grumpy, and disliked individual. Of course, I have not had such great mornings, but I don't let that affect my greeting of a "good morning."

You will begin to feel a little different if you just regulate your thinking, slow down your nervous system, and become aware of your actions. To feel good inside, one must learn to seek validation not through others but within oneself. But first, we must realize that it is not about anyone else; your problems are yours, and you are the only one who can solve them. Healing your insides is not an easy task, but to make your life less morbid and more fruitful, one must try. Your happiness is in your own hands. We have to remind ourselves to go back to the basics and become compassionate humans first.

So now, on my daily walks, I still smile and wish good morning to every passerby, even the ones who choose to ignore me. I realized my mood shouldn't shift just because someone's manners didn't follow them out of bed that morning. My habits won't change because somebody is having a bad morning. It doesn't cost anything to smile, and what a delightful act it is to wish someone a good morning!

I Miss You

A friend recently told me they miss me. I found it amusing; we live nearby. At first, it was humorous; how can you miss me if I don't go away? Nevertheless, it is nice to be told you'll be missed and to know that someone out there will think of you in your absence.

There is a lot in my life I miss. I'm a homebody by nature. I love to travel abroad, but at some point, I'll be sure to get homesick. Inevitably, I miss my children; my heart aches to be with them. What is it about children? I simply need to hear their voices, to feel their presence, and somehow this longing to be with them intertwines them with my heart. But it misses them when they leave.

I miss my family. We had a history, a blood bond, roots, and parents that bound us together like tape. Parents cannot be replaced; they hold a place in your world that leaves a void when they're gone. I miss having them tremendously.

I miss my close friends because they are the few people in this world I chose as my own. I can laugh until my heart's content, I can talk endlessly, and I can shed a tear or two in their presence. I truly miss having an animal beside me, one that follows me around and expects nothing but attention and love. They are the true definition of loyalty, and they show how much they missed you in the manner in which they wait for your return.

After a while of thinking about my friend's remark, it dawned on me that most of us don't want to admit that we miss someone. No one wants to be the first to admit it, either. Speaking our minds at times is hard; keeping feelings inside isn't doing anyone any good. Tomorrow, you may not get that chance. Tomorrow may never come. And all the while we wait for the right time and right place to say how we feel.

If there is magic between two souls, of course, you'll be missed. Spending time with someone is priceless. It's time that we don't have enough of, and time that runs out. So, when you receive it, it becomes valuable and cherished. You'll always remember the one who gave that time to you.

Love starts that way; you start to miss that special person first. Death ends the same way; you miss them when they leave. We teach our children at a young age to share. Not sharing is selfish. Doesn't the same principle apply here? Sharing your feelings doesn't make you weak; it shows you care. It's an act of bravery and compassion.

Thinking about this episode made me realize that missing someone is a lot like love; you can't make someone miss you back. You can't make them miss you as much as you miss them, and that may very well be the root of the silence, of why we hesitate to admit it. What we're scared to know, scared of finding out, is that you weren't missed or loved as much as you thought.

Thank You!

I wrote recently about saying "sorry" frequently, and how we say these words because they've been embedded in us. We have been programmed from childhood to be polite and respectful regardless of our surroundings. We say them without a second thought, and sometimes we don't even mean them. On occasion, though, it's imperative to sit and resonate with the meaning of being thankful. For instance; how many times do we repeat the phrase "thank you"? The repetitiveness and overuse are insane.

Then comes along a season and one day in particular that reminds us that being thankful is not just a meaningful gesture but should be articulated in our way of life. Gifts are for giving, but when we receive in abundance, unwrapped, organic, and meaningful gifts, we should be beyond thankful. More often than not, we disregard them because they are taken for granted. Our life, no matter how tough it may be, is a gift. It's the biggest, most precious gift. As this year comes to a close, I thought long and hard about my accomplishments and how I have tackled this second chance at life. I have so much to be thankful for.

This all may sound mediocre and somewhat mundane, but life is a series of rollercoaster rides that has taught me many valuable lessons very late in life. We spend our whole being searching or running towards a goal or wanting success. I had no such expectations in my life. I didn't know what I wanted or where I was going. I was blindly following and driven by the needs of others. I finally got the chance to choose my path and make my own decisions and not be controlled by people or society. I got a chance to become "me" and work on myself.

I learned that amongst the chaos of obtaining worldly pleasures, we must also seek the will to be secure and confident in our shoes. To be able to realize that not everything in life is a race or a goal, and just seeping through to your inner being is also a success of another magnitude. These are simple things that require only time and your attention, and yet are the very things that are the hardest to obtain. I have become content with being the "organic" me, and I find nothing wrong with that. What you see is what you get; I have no desire to complicate it any longer.

It takes practice not to be moved by your surroundings, letting things go, and just letting them be. Having compassion and some empathy for a fellow human and the will to help whenever possible. To remain positive and content. These very traits are what will leave with you when it's your time to withdraw from this life; everything else will stay, but people will remember you for the person you were. My goal became something of value to myself. I had never thought of life as the story I got to write. To be satisfied with oneself, to accept one's past as a lesson and be willing to maneuver this journey with grace and a sense of accomplishment, to be a role model, and most importantly, to be empathetic and kind.

I'm thankful today for the experiences that made me the person I have become, thankful that I don't need a lot to please me, and thankful that I give myself the time and energy to work through my flaws because I'm worthy, and in return if I can touch just one life with positivity, my existence was worth it. I want to be remembered for the person I am, not for my successes or failures, but to be remembered for my humble heart that gave more than it took. So, I thank you for being a part of my journey, touching it in some way, and giving me a chance to give back to my little galaxy.

Sharing Is Caring

The tomatoes are a little overripe, I realize as I try to glide the knife across them, and they squash and become a mess. I disregard the nuisance and chop at them anyway. The last of my ingredients goes into the bowl, and I feel satisfied that I've allowed myself the time to cook today.

My small but simple kitchen has been replaced by endless gadgets and large workspaces. Conveniently, I realized cooking wasn't my forte, and I adjusted into a fraction of space with astonishing ease. I cooked in the past because I didn't have a choice. I enjoy entertaining and feeding, even cleaning, which pleases me.

Now I wonder why cooking for myself has become such a chore. I'd rather cook when I can share—invite someone over, but it's not always doable. I'm ready to take on the battle for just one other person. The planning and preparation of a wholesome dish for someone to enjoy, there's just some unexplainable satisfaction I gain. I don't need recipes, and gathering ingredients comes with ease now; it makes me believe practice does eventually make perfect. I miss sharing meals. There are times I satisfy my hunger with whatever I can. Other times, I feel I'm worth the effort of whipping up a gourmet meal for myself.

When I was a little girl, I didn't have any interest in cooking. My creations resulted in disasters, and my mother would mourn the loss of her ingredients. My father, on the other hand, was always hard to please when it came to food, but he assured me, next time I'd do better. I'd offer to clean up instead or be the courier from one house to the next, because my parents would share dishes with neighbors. It was my mother who taught me never to return an empty dish. If someone went out of their way to cook for you, the least you can do is appreciate their effort and return the favor. Lucky for the neighborhood, both my parents were good cooks, and they also had big hearts when it came to sharing.

When I traveled with my dad, it wasn't the person selling trinkets that caught his attention, but the person begging for food. He always gave in to hunger. "No one should die of hunger," he'd say. My mother would never close her kitchen. If I were hungry at 10 p.m., she would gladly feed me. They taught me how to make mealtime a group effort. When I moved abroad, she walked me through recipes over the phone. My father would gladly whip up his favorite dishes for me when he visited. He'd say, "I can do better than the restaurants," and to that statement, I'd give in. He disliked the performance one had to display when dining out. "You should be able to taste and share, enjoy a meal without constriction," he'd say. A meal isn't just about exploring the palette, but about the aromas and satisfying a deeper taste; the company, conversations, laughter, and restfulness of unwinding. Take your time to savor every bite.

I watch the sun setting. To balance out the ambience, I pour myself a glass of wine, which pairs well with the music. When one begins to feel comfortable dining alone, that is when you've secured the very essence of being comfortable in your skin. Simple things bring immense pleasures if you can make a little time to appreciate them. We need that time on our side to create some worth for ourselves. It's what we live for and what we work for, isn't it? All we need to survive is two meals a day; yet, for this simple need, we complicate our entire existence.

As I plate my dish and settle down, I give thanks. The solidarity allows a part of you to inhale the gratitude of a meal, but a noisy crowd gathered at your table also satisfies the notion that meals were meant for sharing. Whenever and wherever you can, don't discount sharing a meal, and always be thankful you can.

Take a Break

"Take a break." It's a piece of advice we just spit out, and yet taking a real break from your daily routine is essential for the mind. We need to take it often, in doses, like medication. It's a prescription to release the troublesome knot that begins to tighten. An antidote to an anxious, stressed persona.

Embark on a new territory once in a while. Leave behind the everyday, cumbersome routine for something offbeat. Leave it all behind: your daily timetable, the sound of your morning wake-up call, the need for winding down at the end of a busy day, and the pressure to catch up again. Try freeing your exhausted mind from the endless entanglement and from the people you please. Leave it all behind for some time, and watch what happens.

Not often enough, we try to break the cycle, but we do it for an hour or a day. One must really take a break for some days or weeks, even. It's very much needed, but we hesitate, not because we can't proceed, but because we become apprehensive about the world that might slow down if we were to leave it behind for too long. The disconnect from your usual surroundings helps clear the fog. It's what's been building up in your head, and as it clears, the mind relaxes. The daily grind, the chores and races we run each day, suddenly come to a halt, and you find yourself pondering meaningless worries.

When one travels, one begins to elucidate. Embarking on new shores opens up a wealth of raw, unprocessed thoughts. The new escape and the vibrant surroundings will help to unravel the anxious mind. Novel people and a refreshed landscape will allow you to untangle the trauma of toil. It's amazing how the invigorated soul processes when unfamiliar territory sets in and new lessons transpire. There will always be a connection to the homeland, and you won't forget the solace.

As you sink deeper into the getaway, the load lightens with ease just enough that you can find your way back if need be. If your surroundings are completely new, it takes less time and makes for an easier transition into alleviation. Is it the course of a less-traveled timetable or perhaps the restored palette? Whatever the case, you're traveling a road to a cure and a destination of rejuvenation.

This planet holds so much to see, so much to experience, and once you taste the sweetness of this escape, you will acquire a remedy for your fatigued mind. Before you know it, you will be ready to take on that grind once again, and once again, but not for a while, you will come back to this same space. The unconventional, for another dose of reassurance that a break is a much-needed medication for the mind.

Floating

This is what it must feel like to be in a mother's womb. Warm, safe, free. I long to be back there, unborn, naïve, and innocent. Protected and dependent on the one who birthed me. We never stop growing, yet you can never feel this safe again. Enclosed in your cocoon, no other beings around you, undisturbed, your peaceful place.

A slight breeze touches my bare skin, and I open my eyes to meet the building towering above me. It's rigid and stern, perfect for blocking the sun while I'm floating on my back in the middle of a pool. The water is motionless, just me, the water, time, and my thoughts. Above me, I see the blue that only a beautiful morning can paint. The sky in its deepest shade of cobalt lacks nothing; silently, it beckons my eyes. I follow a few feather-like clouds floating by, and my eyes close once again.

My thoughts catch up with me. When we leave this life, will I feel just like this? Will my soul emerge free and weightless just as I feel at this moment? No burdens to carry, no person to please, no expectations, and no emotions. I hear the early morning birds and the hustle and bustle of daybreak, yet my thoughts seem eluded by my surroundings.

Each day we wake, life unfolds, and we are the ones maneuvering toward the chaos that complicates it. I'm content today. If I feel happy, I'll dance like the waves, and if I feel pain, I prefer to be still like this, and sink into waters where I can let go, but today I'm just content. Happy that my life is unfolding with ease.

The Walk

I walk a lot, alone, outdoors, with my music, nature, and myself. I'm so used to it now, it's become a ritual. It satisfies a hunger within me. One that needs to breathe the air and be sedative to unaccompanied noise. My thoughts run wild, and I get satisfaction from questioning and answering them. During this time, I check out my surroundings and nod to passersby as if to acknowledge my presence.

The fondness I have achieved through this self-care ritual has made me somewhat of a pacified soul. The fresh air clears my head; it clears my lungs, and I can focus clearly. The music only I can hear soothes and calms the agitation that develops from this world that never seems to stop. Music is to me what sand is to the sea. It follows me everywhere; it's what my feelings sound like; it touches me emotionally where words cannot.

Today, I wonder why we are here. Why are we constantly trying to compete as if the race will end without us? Does it even matter? Tomorrow, if I don't wake up, the world will still be spinning without me. Then who am I competing with or even trying to please? I should learn to understand myself, do things for myself, and satisfy my thirst. If I'm content, only then should I consider pleasing another. You see, it is a substance of cause and effect. You are no good to someone else if you are not happy and in a good state of mind. You are no good to your family if you are unwell. You are no good to yourself if your head is filled with hiccups that belong to someone else, complicated obstacles, and limitations. It takes a great deal of courage to acknowledge that you are emotionally unsettled. We bury so much clutter in our minds that it's impossible sometimes to unravel. The road we travel is never smooth, and we fail to look ahead and slow down to avoid the bumps approaching us. Instead, we're so busy dodging the unevenness before us, we don't see the ones coming. So you see, I walk not to avoid the bumps but to be a little more aware of how to deal with them and perhaps take a brief detour—take it slow and easy, dealing with each bump when I get there. I walk to be vigilant and present in my thoughts and my surroundings.

Sent with Love

Just the other day, I was completing a form. As I handed the paper over, I was told I had excellent penmanship. I was taken aback as I hadn't heard this word in years. "Penmanship," the mere art of writing. It was satisfying to know someone noticed my handwriting. I do like to write, and in this digital era, it seems like it's lost its vibe and become something of yesteryear. Why don't we write anymore? Why has it become so hard to plow through the whole process? Writing letters and correspondence by hand, there was just something so authentic about the whole exercise. It seems so primeval now, like an indigenous form of art.

When you handwrite something, your brain has to slow down to meet the speed of your hand. You think clearly, and you translate exactly what is in your thoughts at that exact moment, no shortcuts, no rushing. It's like baking; you can't hurry the process. When you handwrite a letter to someone, it becomes personal and a sentimental archive. It feels special to know that at that moment someone took the time to put pen to paper and write to you. It's a priceless experience for both the writer and the reader.

In my primary years, before the era of the smartphone and email, we had pen pals. Someone in another country with whom you became friends through the exchange of letters. Although a pen pal was someone you never met, but my pen pal was my grandfather. We hardly met; he lived in another country, but our love grew through these letters. We both used all the English we knew and scribbled it on our letters to each other. I remember collecting stamps from all the letters I received, and I treasured my fountain pen like gold.

I moved away to another country, and writing letters remained a large part of my tie with my loved ones. I still send greeting cards today. Yes, a text is much easier, but I hope there are some folks out there, like me, who remain loyal to this irreplaceable technique. It's one of life's little pleasures. I'm reading *The Diary of Anne Frank.* As a child, she handwrote her thoughts, so many penned letters pulled together to publish a whole book. I'm quite certain children today don't even know how to address an envelope; it's sad. Every generation should study the skill of letter writing. Your penmanship doesn't matter as much as the key to just composing a correspondence.

So, I invite you to bring out paper or a greeting card and your favorite pen, sit at a table with a cup of tea, and write to a dear friend or a loved one. Let the words flow. It doesn't have to be an agenda; it could be just because. Let your mind unravel and take in the joy of this exercise. When you come to the end, seal it with some love. Unquestionably, you will feel blissful. There is something undoubtedly special when you see an envelope, hand-addressed to you, and inside you find a handwritten note from someone special, sent with love.

Time Will Tell

I was given three options. I read the text over again. Initially, upon reading it, it amused me. The second glance made me blush. How should I respond? My three options were a result of my stupidity. Option one was a no-brainer. Option two I could deal with, but option three made me feel as if I would be tested. Did I want to be tested? I envisioned the act, and it made me feel other things that I stopped in their tracks.

Our glances met in a group setting, and something strange happened. I'm not sure what it was exactly. An exchange of silent vibrations continued as I struggled to stand upright in my heels. The subtleness of eye contact, the body language, the mutual interest in conversation, or was it just an illusion? I tried to brush it off, but I failed.

I would otherwise have deemed the action rude; he didn't dismiss his phone, but we were strangers, and the phone plays an integral part in filling in the silent queues. I let it go as we went our separate ways following our respective parties. When we were eventually seated, we ended up side by side again. Heat began protruding; I blamed the wine at first. My supple skin brushed against the suit fabric. How could I be so hot just sitting next to fabric? I spoke nonstop as if the night would come to a sudden end. I blamed the wine again, which spoke for me, without thinking. I felt channeling my frequencies in another direction may serve me better. Yet no matter how hard I tried, the affair at hand stood solid.

Such connections and exchanges happen at unexpected moments, and it's these exact moments you feel eluded from your surroundings. I was opposed to such meetings; not only did they not interest me, but I was certain they wouldn't cross my path. Yet when it happened, I was drawn in like a puppy is enticed with a treat.

We parted with an exchange of pleasantries, and that was that. I wasn't aware I was capable of leaving an impression, but I had. I did my due diligence in responding, and here I am, trying to figure out which option to pick because I started meeting number two on the wrong foot. It was awkward to say the least, and now it's payback time. I was given three options to right my wrong. I would have just laughed it off, but playing along gave me something to hold on to until next time. It's the humor that binds us, the playful tug and pull, because life is serious, and when the person on the other end can bring a smile to your face, why not? When you're told they don't want the first time you spoke to be the last time, you're kind of obligated to keep the conversation flowing.

We're opposites, different lifestyles, different upbringings, and perhaps different goals too. Yet in some surprising way, we are very much alike. The subtleness in our similarities is evident; morals, caring, mellow, eager for connection, maybe an adventure, or should I say interested in a disposition of another kind. Above all this, it was the comfort one felt when in the presence of another being. Is that not also a key to attraction? I was being exposed to a sense of safety, and I found a fondness for the net.

The matter at hand is still under much debate. The options will continue to weigh, and in the presence of the evidence, the outcome will reveal itself. Time will only tell what comes from the pleasant organic bond we hold. Our paths crossed for a reason, and should it lead to a destination, well, that is yet to be seen. No matter the outcome, it will always be remembered because you never forget how someone made you feel.

Giving Away a Son

It is a happy occasion, and this maternal overload of love running through my veins is normal; I tell myself this on repeat. But just like most things in my life, no one showed me how to cope. No one taught me how to navigate these feelings.

My boys are grown up now, and I don't have a daughter. I tried to understand the difference between nurturing a daughter and a son. The culture I was brought up in definitely defined the difference between the two. I'm not sure if I would have treated a daughter any differently. I would provide the same nurturing I gave my boys. Protected her, loved her, and showed her respect and affection.

When a daughter marries, you lose a part of her. One day, she leaves your space and enters another. She becomes someone else's, and you feel somewhat abandoned. I know this because I was a daughter. I watched my parents who dealt with the emotions they fought with a separation.

Today I stand here as my son has taken the first important step in his long-term relationship; he's engaged. The hours of planning and thought, the commitment, and the love he holds for her are all packed in the ring she proudly wears.

I try hard to swallow the heaps of emotions that are blocking my ability to be present. I wasn't supposed to feel like this; torn apart. I'm happy for him, of course. I want the best for him, for them both. Then why do I feel like I'm losing something that I held so dear to my heart? I'm losing a part of him, as if he's leaving my space, he's becoming someone else's, and now I'll have to wait in line for his attention. I'm feeling the same feelings parents with daughters feel. Emotionally drained, scared, concerned, and abandoned.

I experienced some of these emotions when he left for college; they became stronger when he moved out into his own home. Now, I feel as if I'm giving him away for good, just as if I were giving away a daughter.

I gather myself together and continue admiring him from a distance. My, he has grown. The little boy I carried now walks his own walk. His confident demeanor, strong handshake, and wealth of knowledge no doubt awarded him his place in life. I think of how lucky she is to have such a well-grounded gentleman in her life. Someone I nurtured, taught, and loved. I know he will take care of her. In the end, she is the one who won him over. I don't discount the fact that she deserves him, but a part of me will always lose him to her.

I watch her gleaming smile, and I tell myself she, too, is someone's daughter; she, too, is leaving their space to start a new life. Her parents will give her away, and she'll walk beside my son. The cycle of life will repeat with them, too. One day, they, too, will feel these exact emotions.

Unfortunately, these are the cards we parents are dealt. We sacrifice the things we love the most. Just like her ring, my heart will hold his entire childhood, the years of commitment, the endless love, and the mounds of blessings I wish for them both. In the end, when you let them fly on their own, there really is not much difference between a son and a daughter. I want to believe that I am not losing my son, but in fact gaining the daughter I never had.

Going Home

I see the white Tesla turn the corner and begin collecting my luggage so it can be placed into the boot. The driver, a smart middle-aged gentleman, is pleasant and makes room to fit both pieces strategically among his belongings.

I get into the vehicle and exchange pleasant words about the unusually warm weather here in London. While he finishes a call, I text my cousin to tell her I'm on my way to the airport.

Ahmad is from Lebanon. He looks at me through the rearview mirror to ask where I'm headed for my holiday, and I laugh. I remind him he picked me up from a hotel and then end with, "I'm going home." His cute smile is followed by another question, "So where's home? Because you seem like you're from around here."

I'm silent for a minute, mainly to digest how many times I've changed the place I call home. "I am in fact from here, but I live elsewhere now," I add. My statement intrigues him more.

As I grab my seatbelt to get buckled in, I contemplate, had I had a seatbelt just like this throughout my life, perhaps I would have been safer. Instead of always trying to tackle life, I could have played it safe. But then I would not have ventured into new territory.

My thoughts get disrupted. "Why so far away?" Ahmad asks.

I tell him, I wanted a fresh start. "I like it there," I reply. He tells me that while he doesn't know me, he can tell I'm happy, so it must be a good decision. "I am happy," I tell myself. It's the happiest I've been, the most peaceful my life has been, and although I miss my origins and the few people I have to travel to meet. I wouldn't have it any other way.

This is the third time in my life I have made a home in a foreign place. For some, I'm brave, and for others, I should have stayed put. While people were speculating, I realized in my midlife, home is where my peace lay and where I gained freedom.

I grew up in the suburbs of a small town in England, where the rows of brick houses seemed anything but appealing. Lampposts lined the street, and everyone's back garden was manicured to their own tastes. I grew accustomed to traveling on foot in the rain and wind. I played with all the children on my street; I lived a simple childhood. Everything was so much easier and simpler then. We didn't know what stress was and what adulting entailed. We lived for fun, and it cost nothing but time.

In my late teenage years, I moved to what was then considered the world's superpower, the US of A. I made a home near the capital and lived a different lifestyle from that of my humble beginnings. I drove amongst the sedans on the open freeways, experienced all four seasons in the extreme. I grew up quickly, and distance set in; marriage kept me apart from

loved ones, work chained me, and children took up my life, giving birth to a family and building an empire. I became engulfed in the rat race.

And then in my midlife, I left that life and moved away to another metropolitan city. One where the sun never forgets to shine. The vibrancy here showed me what life was really about. It taught me to slow down, live a little, and become someone I was meant to be. I became wiser, more confident, and secure; I found solidarity here next to the ocean.

I still wish my loved ones were close, but then I'd miss out on the excitement, traveling, catching up, and taking in the very essence of rekindling and being missed.

Ahmad seemed very interested in my being single so late in life. Our conversation was geared towards the irrational decisions we made in our younger days. "I don't regret anything," I tell him. "I learned a lot from my life, and I refuse to say my experiences were mistakes." My life is simple now, but for Ahmad, I was living some kind of adventure. I listen as he talks about me from the very little he knows, his reasoning of how bold he thinks I am.

My life took me full circle. At one point, I felt as if I had lived an entire lifetime. Coming back to a place I had left so many years ago overwhelmed me with memories, a lot of them sad. I reminisced about my childhood. It's funny how time changes a place. Now I'm in a home where I wish I had more time, because I have so much more of life to experience. "My home is where I can be the best version of myself," I tell him. Ahmad shares his family life, and I tell him I'm jealous; he tells me he wishes he had my freedom. I remind him, "To gain something, we have to give up something, and the grass is always greener where you water it."

As I say goodbye, he wishes me the best of luck. I joke and tell him I'm only going home. He replies, "Not all of us have a happy home to go to. You have taught me a lot in one car ride. Keep smiling, and a few good wishes never hurt anyone."

PART II

Lessons from the Past

Memories, reflections, nostalgia, and learning - looking back isn't about regret, it's about honoring who we were and what shaped us.

- Never Meant to Be — Page 39
- A Toast — Page 42
- I Watched — Page 44
- If It Were That Easy — Page 46
- Is Two Better than One? — Page 48
- I Forget — Page 50
- Broken Family — Page 52
- Nothing Lasts Forever — Page 55
- Murder of the Soul — Page 57
- What Death Sounds Like — Page 60
- Fairytales Belong in Books — Page 62
- Candlelight Dinner — Page 65
- The Crown Jewel — Page 67
- Secrets — Page 69
- Silence — Page 72

Never Meant to Be

I stare out of the floor-to-ceiling windows; the view never gets old. A whole world passes by, a world that never stops. No matter what happens, life carries on, and everyone manages. "It was never meant to be anyway." These are the exact words I should say, but I'm speechless.

I turn and look at the chiseled face with indented lines I know so well. It is also gazing out at nothingness. Something has changed. There's a moment of silence scattered here and there, like pieces of a jigsaw puzzle. We tried to brainstorm and put the pieces where they belong, but they became misaligned—just like our relationship, which remains incomplete.

It was never meant to be, and even though I longed for the day that things might change in my favor, I knew very well that nothing would. It's not healthy to ponder over "what ifs." The rules were laid out in the beginning, and knowing the results, I played the game. It was wonderfully played at first, no matter how short it was.

I was stunned at how I became so likable and adored. Someone's behavior toward me opened up a side of me I never knew existed. It took time, and now the very person I opened up to is becoming estranged. This person taught me how to be comfortable with myself and revealed how interesting and intelligent I am. They guided me into a realm of stoicism. I don't think I fully understood how my secure, organic simplicity was attractive and appealing to this individual.

This person accepted me for who I was, not who they wanted me to be. It was the intensity of our conversations and our agreeable differences that provided me with an environment to voice my opinions. I fit like a glove when we bonded; nothing felt out of place. I never knew one could become so naturally comfortable with another person. We laughed, confided in each other, debated, and even became upset, but we knew how to accept our differences and move forward with respect.

Some people cross your path and leave marks—not small blemishes, but an impact so profound that it alters your world. As they journey on, they teach you the lessons you must learn, then begin their exit. You stand in a trance and wonder if your life will ever be the same again. A tear escapes, and out of fear of more following, I get up and walk toward the window.

It's a vast world out there with billions of people, I tell myself. I will find another. But will I? There are no regrets, just sadness.

The thought of losing what could have been makes me shudder because it was easy and comfortable. Like home, it made me feel safe, and deep down, I knew it would shelter me. That feeling of safety was all it took. Except I forgot; I was hurt right at the beginning when the rules were laid out. I continued playing a game I would never win, all while knowing nothing would change. So, my decision to move on became not just a reality, but a choice based on the fact that there was nothing here for me to grow on.

I look back at the sad face and glazed hazel eyes. No matter how badly I want to replace this tear with the laughter that erupted effortlessly between us, or how badly I want to be held and hold on, I know it will only lead to heartache. I feel like the flower bud in a vase that wants to bloom in all its glory but is left to wilt because it needs to be nurtured constantly.

Finally, and so late in life, I had found my safe space—an embrace that could heal, an ear that would listen, and a partner in crime who never questioned my insanity. No one won this game; we gave up before it ended. I wanted to beg for another chance, but instead, I managed to force the words out: "It was never meant to be anyway."

A Toast

I watch the ripples in the pool water as they bounce to the mellow beats playing in the background. The mountain breeze brushes past now and again as if to signal its presence. The happy couple greet the guests as they trickle in one by one. It's a pre-wedding gathering, the scenery, a beautiful rooftop view of fields, hills, and open air.

I observe the excitement. It is exciting to announce to the world your chosen partner for life. Celebrating with your loved ones and hoping that the ritual of this matrimony is as perfectly executed as they had dreamed it would be. So far, nothing is out of place.

The breathtaking venue holds centuries of history, where old architecture meets a new generation. Stone structures house the silk and linens. A finely manicured landscape and the rustic surroundings will help make an abundance of cuisine more palatable. The wooden beams and ancient ruins will unite this couple for life. The rich landscape and delicate florals will intertwine the ceremony, a ritual of vows that will encompass togetherness.

As I celebrate the marriage of two lives, two cultures, and two families, a deeper understanding begins to fill my thoughts. In the end, nothing matters really, except that the road that brought these two souls together remains strong and solid. May it be resilient enough to withstand all the difficulties a marriage faces. It's smooth enough to make the ride that much more meaningful.

I selected a few words to engrave on a greeting for them. I know I did well when I brought a tear to their eyes. Words have more impact than we can imagine. Blessings carry far more weight than plain wishes. I hope their togetherness lasts a lifetime. The words flowed as I wrote; I hope they lift one another and walk beside each other always, because isn't that what marriage is really about? After the day is over, they will have only each other. No other will walk in their shoes, and no one will endure this marriage. They will share their happiness and fears. No secrets, no pretense, no lies. We forget that part, the part where we commit to eternity. No one can know exactly what the meaning of this bond holds except the two of them.

I console the groom's grandmother as she becomes emotional; it's her eldest grandchild. Deep down, I know, part of her tears cry for someone else. Her soulmate is being missed today. The unity of their marriage ended with a broken heart. I'm witnessing her devotion as she lived through her marriage until the very end. Some of us don't make it that far. We forget marriage means two people unite through ups and downs, together for a lifetime. She's blessed to be witnessing her grandchild exchanging vows, a privilege few attain. Life is a gamble; for every gain there is a loss. It's this balance that needs to stay afloat through this marriage.

As we raised our flutes to toast, I silently blessed the happy couple with strength and understanding for a blissful ride into the future. One where they walk beside each other always. This selfless journey they're about to embark on may be a bond of trust, respect, and support. A toast to new beginnings and happy endings!

I Watched

I watched my life go by. At times, I stood still and I let it pass. Just like the water in a flowing river, it passed by me, never to return. It flowed into greater and deeper depths. Other times, I didn't want to watch, but the unswerving episodes immobilized me. I watched happy moments leaving so swiftly. I watched reality kick into my fairytale life.

I watched my mother's tears fall down her rosy cheeks as she bid me farewell one last time. I stood motionless as her translucent complexion was ushered into another dimension. I watched fate deal the cards for me, and society showed me my place, and people assigned my duties. I watched the love I gifted separate into morsels, and the love I deserved was handed to another. I watched the battlefield, but I didn't understand that it was my war. I watched from a distance as the pack conspired, and I fought my battle alone. I watched people take over my space. I watched a loved one wither away. I longed to be closer, but distance can be cruel.

I watched as I feathered my own nest. I watched the innocent face as it came out from inside me. I watched how it grew, how the transformation went from beautiful to bold. I gave them wings, and then I watched them fly. I watched how time didn't stand still, even for a moment, and I could savor the drops of my happiness. I saw my humble abode become empty and lifeless.

I watched the moon when the nights wouldn't end, and I watched the clouds float by when my body gave in. I watched myself dig a hole, and then I watched as I filled it back. I watched myself walk a tightrope, and then I watched myself fall. There were so many hands to help, but not one reached out. I watched as backs were turned, and bonds were cut. My bleeding heart ached, my insides turned raw, and I stood and watched it all. The words were hurled at me as I sat in silence, motionless, unable to respond. I felt the pillow soak up my tears, so there would be no evidence left of the crime.

I was confused as to why I was never enough. I watched the silence on the road I walked, and then turned to run from the noise. When power and money both destroyed my surroundings, I watched myself become humbler. I watched as I tried to bridge gaps for relationships and hold up the fort. I have been a pillar, a shoulder, and a punching bag. I have also watched myself become depleted by the very thing that I showered. I watched my love vanish; it just wasn't enough, it never was.

I watched the consequences of being a woman, the struggle of a wife, the toil of a sister, the sacrifice of a mother, the devotion of a daughter, and the loyalty of a friend. I watched the adoration of a child and the goodwill of a stranger. I embraced the kindness of a friend, and I felt the endearment of a passerby.

I watched the sadness in my eyes turn to a glow on my face. I watched peace enter my mind and friends enter my space. I watched myself become fearless, strong, and compassionate. I watched my past without regret and unyielding love, and how I became who I was meant to be. I watched that little girl inside me give birth again. I watched in amazement as I survived the life that passed by. I stood still, and it passed, but I couldn't watch myself fail.

If It Were That Easy

I realized it only when distance set us apart, how I took you for granted. When you were no longer in this world, I realized the importance I hadn't given you. You gave me life, and I realized what that meant when you lost yours.

The one who taught me to walk and to speak, what do I say to you now that you are gone? To the one who went without, to give me more, where do I go to get back even a piece of you? At which temple do I light a candle for your soul? Where do I go to bow my head for forgiveness? Would you hear me if I told you how much it hurts? Years have gone by, yet the cry and my tears have remained the same. How I long for your embrace, how I long for you to call my name the way only you did. Your absence, I still feel it today. Time hasn't healed anything really, it's just made me realize that everything else around me could have waited, but you were so much more important because there wasn't enough time left.

After you left, I longed to be a mother. I longed to hold something so close, something to call my own. I'm a mother now. Only when I became one did I realize the power of a matriarch. Only a mother stays awake all night seeking comfort for her child. Only a mother hurts when her child is in pain. It's when she carries her unborn child that she becomes fearless; that is also when another avatar within her takes birth. The one who will lie and cry for her own will do anything to shield them. Today, when they are grown, my maternal strength remains, and I will continue to protect. A mother does the little things and the unimaginable, and yet we go about our lives as if it is our struggle alone. No man realizes the depth of our pain, and yet it is man himself who is born from us. We are the ones who give birth to the future; what we leave behind is our legacy.

Don't get me wrong, my father also held love in his heart for me, but my mother held the love of the universe. He knew how to love me, but my mother knew how to give her life for me. He showered me with blessings and prayed for me, but my mother would have fought the universe for me. Her one tight embrace didn't have a chance against his one withered hug. If being a mother were that easy, every father could have become one.

Is Two Better than One?

There will be times in your life when you will barely be alive, and times when you realize that surviving on your terms is better than living an unhappy life on someone else's terms. Some of us are afraid of being alone, and some are afraid that we may end up alone. Yet when we die, we leave alone, and when we come into this world, we also come alone.

Spending time alone makes one more vulnerable to overthinking. We become susceptible to isolation, and depression sets in, or so that is the perception. We have to learn to manage our thoughts. We weren't made to be isolated, and yet ironically, isolation means you get peace. But were we meant to be bonded with another individual for life?

Is having a life companion just a matter of the mind, a comfort that we believe is a need? Is it a ritual society pushed into our minds? Does the need of another person really complete you as an individual, or does it make you weak? Do two people create a stronger bond, or do you lose your individuality? Is two really better than one?

Two people, if together, should create a bond stronger than what the eye sees. For some time, I suppose we do. Then life happens, time passes, years go by, and we change. These circumstances bring different outcomes. We begin to drift apart, other things become important, it's all too inevitable.

We forget that two people together should also be individuals. They should have an identity completely of their own. We begin to morph into each other, and that results in distaste. We should be allowed to grow and change as a unit. We stunt the very growth that needs to happen because we become selfish. We begin to take for granted the very thing that was once treasured.

A strong bond equals compromises and loyalty, and an unselfish mind. Yet are we completely honest with what we hide in our minds, and are our thoughts always aligned? It's this false sense of accountability we have no control over; what is it that really goes on in another's mind? We don't reveal everything, do we? Over time, we grow, and growth brings change, so if you begin to grow at different levels, your paths will most certainly be unaligned.

Alone time is necessary; it's medicine for the mind. Recharging and realigning your life, sifting through the things that actually matter to you as an individual. Spending time alone helps you work through yourself; it assists in bringing out the issues that stunt your growth. Alone time helps you clear a fogged memory bank and cleanse your persona. You begin to dissect thoughts and the reasons behind your actions, and you will begin to compartmentalize your life. Being alone makes you understand that you alone can be enough. It doesn't mean you have failed in a relationship; it means you became stronger as an individual.

I'm sure there is a match out there for everyone, a so-called "soulmate," but even the word "mate" translates to friend. Every bond begins as a friendship, a companion that shares mutual affection. If you find that friend, help them help you. Be a union of the hearts and one that not only loves but supports, pushes, and encourages your growth. One that gives and takes equally, but most importantly, one that gives you space to be a better person for you both.

I Forget

I'm beginning to forget what you feel like. I'm leaving behind all the feelings of discontent as I slide into this new phase. I forget why I was there, why your presence didn't allow me to stray from the uneasiness of your space. I'm beginning to forget what made me feel like you were worth the wait. Why did my patience overrule my will to want something I thought was unattainable? I'm beginning to forget the pain I endured. My limbs have forgiven the brutality of your words. The words that displaced me made me feel unworthy, and because time didn't allow me to flow with the winds, I succumbed to your seasons of bitterness.

They say time heals, but really it doesn't heal a thing. Time passed, and with each passing year, I started to forget a little more. Time teaches us not to give up. We never completely heal. New desirable circumstances become just that, more desirable than what you leave behind. I've allowed myself now to shed the layers of wounds your impact had upon me. Yesterday I hung on to them; self-pity doesn't allow you to let go. Self-pity demolishes your will to break free.

A mere image, a spoken word, a passing scent, anything familiar can take me back and make me feel the discomfort once again. There was a time when I felt it with so much intensity. But slowly, I began to forget what suffering was. I'm loosening the links that tied me down.

No matter how long you live in someone's shadow, you can break free. We don't give ourselves the credit we deserve. The courage we have lives dormant, and so you continue to follow the path of subdued resentment until one day you realize the shadow you follow has no soul, therefore no heart. You were blindly giving to someone who doesn't deserve your heart.

I'm here to tell you, there is a way to break free. You need the will to fight, to be able to unchain all that's weighing you down. It isn't dishonorable to be a little selfish. It is commendable to have the strength to walk your own walk. It is admirable to know your worth. That is how, one day, you learn to forget the pain you endured. You can battle the demon that kept you from living, and when you taste the sweetness of freedom and this beautiful life, you will slowly shed the wounds and begin to forget.

I'm learning that, little by little, letting go is fruitful. I'm embarking on a journey of self-worth and making space for my own portrait, replacing each tear with a smile. Replacing the discontent with hope, replacing the unjust with some clarity. Time did teach me how to live again. A different kind of love gave birth within me, and slowly but surely, everything became better without you. One fine day, I'll forget what you made me feel like.

Broken Family

"There is no such thing as a broken family." I read this today, and I let it sink in for a while. I'm not sure if I digested the statement correctly. Broken families do exist. My first immediate family ended up broken; it happened in my youth, a result of a sudden death. I was always a family girl, right in the center of the circle. Everything in my life revolved around family. It was a circumstance beyond anyone's control, and yet the result tore my family apart. My second family, through marriage, also resulted in a broken family from divorce. So this phenomenon I was reading wasn't resonating with me at all.

The article went on to say, "Family is not determined by papers and documents, families are made with ties to the heart." To some degree, I agree here, but papers and documents ultimately determine the fate of a family, and ties to the heart can also be broken.

No family is perfect; they each have flaws. It's the characters that make up a family that are different. Not everyone thinks alike or sees alike; it's this makeup that can never be equal. When push comes to shove, they all come together as a family should. Yet each family member has their own agenda, because we are different even though we are cut from the same cloth. When breaking began, it was because I stepped away from my position as peacemaker. Disappointment seeped through those seams, but no one noticed. I realized everyone satisfies their own hunger, and in my time of need, backs were turned, and I was left abandoned.

I continued to work damn hard to make sure that my relationships didn't change, no matter how hard the forces were against me. Deplorable habits set in, and I nurtured them, knowing it was hard work. I wasn't about to let a piece of paper enforce how the family was now divided or broken. Some souls gladly sat perched in an uncomfortable seat because getting up meant they'd break the family. I can relate. I did just that, until I couldn't take it anymore. My decision to leave a so-called "throne" broke the family. It's beyond devastation, maneuvering through torn bonds, especially where children are involved.

There is a difference between dysfunctional families and those that are broken. I'm aware now, I belonged to dysfunctional families that eventually broke. Ones that didn't want the best for each other, disloyal ones that didn't support each other, and apparently ones that didn't love either. So there were no ties of the heart; it was all loose strings and all one-sided. I held on because I believed in the unity of a family bond.

No one ever died from a divorce, but just like marriage or parenting, it's a direct result of a family union. It was my small idiosyncrasies that made me believe I was to blame because I failed. When it is the facts that say it all. You should get out of a relationship what you put into it. If you cut ties from the heart, the result is being torn apart, and if you make ties from the heart, it becomes a connection.

Family to me used to mean togetherness, blood ties, unspoken promises, roots, support, and love. At times, I set aside my feelings and rekindle the ties to the heart only to see them break again. Family shouldn't be work but a beautiful, easy union of the hearts. It shouldn't leave a distaste; you shouldn't feel a burden. My family now are people who chose to walk by my side or have somehow made it into my life, made an effort, and stayed with me. We are not linked by parents or blood. No document exemplifies our bond, and like the quote affirms, "My friends became the family I chose."

I concluded that this article didn't tell the real truth about what damage a broken family can really do, or even what a broken family actually is. I didn't care to finish it because no matter how much of it I read, my experiences spoke louder. Broken families do exist. They exist because we have no choice. Individuals tied through blood confirm a bond; there is no option. You either make it work or you step aside, but it doesn't mean you can't create another solid union with people you choose to be your family.

Nothing Lasts Forever

During a recent trip, I found a hidden coffee shop. The board read "Good things never last forever." I'm not going to lie, curiosity drew me in, and I have to say I was pleasantly surprised.

It was small, quaint, and chic. The white-washed interior was decorated with green from a few plants, and everything from the floor to the countertops and even the serving ware was made of marble, porcelain, or some kind of stone in all shades of white. The tag line shone brightly in rose gold above the counter. Each time I looked up, it reminded me how true it was; good things never last forever. This moment will not come back, and neither will the time that has passed.

I paused to sip my perfect cup of coffee from this delightful stone mug in this unusually attractive hole-in-the-wall cafe. This time came to be cherished; it won't last. Relationships don't even last forever. Some memories do stick with you, but for the most part, they too fade. You can try and rebuild the same scenarios, but something will have changed. We change, our minds change, and our likes and dislikes also take a turn.

In this moment, I also realized bad things do not last forever either. Bad times, worries, stress, they also have their limited time with us. I can resonate with those because I have had my fair share of experiences. We hold on to them sometimes more than we need to, because moving on seems harder. We often forget that good thoughts guide us through and pave the way for us to move forward.

I feel blessed that I have made it this far. It's important to be true to yourself to accept yourself, whether in your own cocoon or part of a circle. Things could turn out differently for all of us in a matter of minutes. Tomorrow is a mere fragment of our imagination. Yesterday is what has happened, whether good or bad. We learn lessons every single day. People come and go in our lives for a reason. The trends we follow, the icons we idolize, even the facades we carry, are temporary; what's permanent is who you are today, your very existence, this very minute.

I learned to be thankful, mainly because so much went missing in my life, yet so much came to me later in my life. I'm learning to let go and to accept. It is hard to think of the positives when everything is wrong, when your soul is lost. So with time, I learned it's better to let go and live a little more. I invite the good vibes in and, in turn, let the positivity glow. I began by immersing myself in little things that brought me joy. Time is so precious, but your presence is even more important. I believe I was drawn here to this very spot so this very lesson could be instilled in me once again; be thankful for life, because nothing lasts forever.

Murder of the Soul

You could say it was murder. A crime that never saw justice. What name would I have given this case? I often visualized myself sitting in the courtroom. Yes, I'd have a case, the narcissist versus the empath, but would justice be served? Where would I start to convince the jury that I became a victim? It was a crime, a murder of my benevolent soul. But we merciful ones always lose—we get abused and mistreated, thrown aside, and left to pick up the pieces after someone's egotistical and arrogant demeanor ruthlessly oppresses our ability to function normally.

So I took it upon myself to defend the other party. Because I have now read every inch of the book they wrote. I know exactly how to pull off a seamless entanglement, how to turn a lie into temporary forgiveness, and how to create a web that slowly strangles. I'm aware now how to manipulate feelings and how to stab with emotional assaults. I know how to drive someone into a black hole and how to devalue an innocent mind. I know how to make them believe everything they said had no relevance. I could feed them lies and make them think they were the ones who were going crazy. I could walk the grounds holding all the power, making them feel so small as if they couldn't exist without me. I could slaughter one's self-esteem, mistreat and misuse them, yes, I studied the entire book.

I'd defend the opposing side. There is no reason to play victim here; I'd win this case for them. I can prove how, even with proof, you can get away with murdering an empathic soul.

I've fought all my life; my values and beliefs were never extreme, but perhaps too complicated for the average person to understand. There was that demure side to me that consoled, cared, helped, nurtured, and understood. The very traits that were used and abused. Then, as if I had not known it, I was awakened to the fact that my life was not my own. It was dissected by people who took advantage of me, and one person in particular took it to the extreme.

The law says you need proof; you are innocent until proven guilty. If you act in self-defense, you still need to prove your statement. Do they know some acts of self-defense turn into self-sabotage? The very crime that goes unpunished is the same crime that eats away at our organs. It's the raw insides that you'd see if one dared cut me open. It was the record of indecent bullying that played on repeat in my mind. It was the disloyal hand that led me into a world where I began trusting no one. The suffocation drowned me, and I became a lifeless puppet that lost feeling and all hope.

So, would I have a case? It would be my word against theirs, because emotional abuse, anxiety disorder, traumatic chaos, mental disarray, and depression are not seen by the naked eye. They are felt and when you begin to lose the feeling, parts of you become numb. How do you explain that? It's then you are alone. I couldn't even convince myself that I was being held captive. My facade was real, the sinless face, it was my defense mechanism and yet my insides bled to death silently. Was I silenced or ushered into silence? It makes no difference. They use that side of you, the one that they hold the most power over. Belittling and condescending blows that continue to be thrown. What is it about us? We make ourselves believe that we can fix all the wrongs and everyone deserves a chance, sometimes, third and fourth until we tire ourselves out. We choose to stay because we are loyal, faithful, and loving. Then that choice becomes a life sentence because we begin to believe there is no way out and the guilt of even thinking such eats away at us.

At the end of my closing statement, I'd cry with all my heart and let them know this is the person that couldn't be saved. I was the victim of narcissistic abuse; it was my empathic soul that was murdered. Without a doubt I'd win this case for them. There was never any justice but there was definitely a murder.

What Death Sounds Like

At that moment when I sat with death, I understood so much of life. It wasn't as though I hadn't experienced this bitter episode before. I was young and naïve then, perhaps I didn't grieve enough, but this time it made sense. I sat bedside watching the same man leaving the world that he brought me into. As I crumbled and he lay unaware, I teared in isolation, but my cries went unheard. I pleaded for his life, but death was stronger.

He left me with deep somber thoughts. It was then I felt the ache, when I had him in his entirety, I should have. Isn't it during those days of despair we remember all the "I should haves" we purposely disregarded? The regret sinks into our grief. Throughout my life he gave me advice and now after he left is when I understood his lessons.

This time I understood my purpose. This time around death showed me, my life is in fact limited. It was death that showed me that surviving isn't enough; you have to live. You are worth every breath you breathe; you are worthy of every second that passes. Being humble and comfortable are your successes. He showed me over and over again and now when he lay humbly and comfortably, I realized what he meant.

Death showed me things will stay, but people will leave. The tug of war between what's yours and mine will eventually kill one of us. It showed me to be a bigger person. So, isn't it better to be prepared? To let them know every day, to share your heart and tell them how they are loved by you. In the end when nothing else matters, you matter. I mattered. He gifted me this life, and so this life matters.

What doesn't matter are our wants and needs, greed and vengeance. It's the hate that poisons us and when you can't see past your ego, it is then you begin to sink. I have to rise above all that.

This death showed me that it's okay to speak and console and share and be open. Why must you die in silence? Why must you die in shame and embarrassment? Feel your own pain instead of running from it and covering up the lesions. Share your pain. I didn't know his pain; he didn't share his suffering. I never knew and so it remains an unknown part of his life.

Flowers lie in abundance at your tomb; no one speaks ill. I, too, want to be worthy of fresh flowers and sweet words, but while I'm alive. I want to do good, and so I decided to forsake the grudges and try to forgive. I decided I want to live in peace, so I may leave a legacy of a kind heart. Because I fell mindlessly in the path of convulsion, I had to die just a little to know how to rise again.

This life will carry on with or without me. "Make time," he told me. "Time for all the items on the bottom of your list." He told me to take time to do things that put a smile on my face. "Be happy, time will pass anyway," he said. "Live your life, it's the only one you have." I didn't understand that nothing lasts forever, until he was taken away right before me. He didn't put up a fight. I fought for him until I realized he was ready to leave me behind.

Death taught me that in the end, it's not what he left me, it's what he told me. This time, I understood why I was here and my purpose for living. So, as I tell his stories, and there are many, I'm reminded, in the end, we all become part of a story. We have to decide if that story is worth reciting.

Fairy Tales Belong in Books

I can't watch abuse, even on television. I can't watch horror, and I could never physically hurt anyone. I never hit my children. Discipline to me was a verbal form of communication. Yes, I've screamed and shouted. After all, I am human. My life experiences have taught me how to remain calm through storms. A lot of what makes up me, stems from my childhood. I'm not sure how many of you have had counseling, but they always start off questioning your childhood. It's this process of introspection that will broaden your understanding as to why you behave the way you do. It's the wrongs that happened, the things we witnessed, and the emotions we felt that mold us into the adults we become.

The aftereffects of my departure from a marriage left uneasiness, a bad taste, if you will, for my children. After decades of trying, things fell apart for me. My children are grown up and although they supported me, what I didn't realize is that no matter what the age, children will hurt. In the process of trying to make the right decision for myself, I've hurt them more than I thought was possible.

Like every parent, I wanted a fairytale life for them. One where the grass is always green and the sky blue. Unknowingly, I tainted their perfect upbringing, but then, was it perfect if their mother was unhappy? If I could change it, I would in a heartbeat. I'd bring back the sunshine and white clouds. No mother wants her offspring to suffer in any way. What they didn't realize is, when those gray clouds formed, I too wept. The same mother that protected them 24/7 during their entire youth is the same mother that would protect them today. I did just that for decades. I silently lived an unhappy life for the sake of the family circle.

Sadly, I failed to protect them from separation and a malfunctioning family. I failed to protect them from distance and a loving home. You only see what is right in the moment and we act on it. A distorted vision won't bring clarity when an unjust situation is emotionally absorbed. You don't see the long-term effect it will have, because those waves haven't hit the shore yet.

So, in my anguish, I began reluctantly to walk the yellow brick road. I concluded to realize that no matter how perfect their world may seem, every child will have a story to tell. Just as I have episodes from my youth, disfigured chapters, and unanswered questions. No child is immune to chaos and turmoil, no childhood is a perfect children's story, and no parent is really a superhero. Parents are real people wanting to be superheroes. They are humans with an instinct to shield and secure. Children, however, are an enigma. In a paradox, they can feel the energy, and they sense the vibes. They know. They know things we think we can hide from them, they know how to read their parents, and they know how not to rock the boat. They also know when things are wrong.

You don't start a family wanting a bitter future for your children, you don't have them in the hopes of neglecting and harming them. I write children's stories, and these stories talk to me about the roles mothers and fathers play. We do everything possible with what we know and what we have at the time. It's not a punishable crime to play with the cards we are dealt. We shouldn't be punished for wanting to make the sky blue for them and the grass green for us.

Yet, we do sacrifice to make it a perfect world for our children, but we cannot protect them from life itself. It's unwarranted for them to grow up in a bubble immune to life and its challenges. We also don't have a manual to tell us what page to turn to when things go haywire. These wrongs, the hurdles, the disappointments, this is what will make them who they are. The wrongs will hopefully define how right they can make it; this is what life unknowingly teaches us. In the end, every child will grow up to be a slightly stronger version, because to some degree they were exposed to those challenges and because fairytales only exist in books.

Candlelight Dinner

I straighten my hair as the gentle breeze brushes it while I step out of the golf cart. It's a warm night, and I can smell the ocean as I approach it. I feel the salty, humid heaviness that settles over the sand as night begins to fall. I'm led along a cobbled path, and my dress starts to cling to me. The unease in the air makes it hard for me to stay composed. The ocean sounds clearer now, and when I reach the edge of the sand, my eyes meet a sight seen only in movies: that unreal, stretched-out romantic scene.

In the distance, a canopy glows with what seems like a million bulbs. White sheer drapes hang from a delicately lit chandelier surrounding a small white table, with two chairs on either side, wrapped with white bows as if ready to be gifted. Tall candle sticks sit elegantly on the table, glowing as if they are the stars of the night. Lanterns of all sizes encircle the area, framing this perfect scene against the deep blue night sea, with stars shining brightly above, complementing the moment.

For a minute, I get lost in the view, but a wave of melancholy spreads through me, reminding me this is yet another attempt to silence my own thoughts. It's another carefully crafted manipulation. I close my eyes, making sure I'm fully present, that this isn't just another dream.

We sit, we dine, he speaks, I listen. I try to engage, to smile, but the truth is, once devotion leaves your heart, it rarely comes back no matter how hard you try. You can pretend, but the pain lingers. The somber sound of the ocean pulls at broken strings in my chest. I take a sip of champagne to ease the lump in my throat. I look away to stop the tears, knowing deep down that the night will end unfairly.

I make small talk to divert the conversation from where it's headed. I know where it's going, and I beckon it back. I no longer want to hold his hand, wear the ring, or be here. I think to myself, what a waste of such a beautiful evening, a perfect picture. It could have been a work of art—had it not been stained with pain. The canvas could have shown how we grew old together. A few wrong strokes, and the colors ran.

I tried to fix it, but you and I still see the flaws—where it all went wrong and how it will never make it to the gallery. While I painted my perfect story, you kept erasing the meaningful parts. I grew tired of fixing those strokes, and now, when I'm exhausted, you find the time to create your own art. It's too late now. If only we could start over with a blank canvas, but then… would I choose the same artist?

A lavish, intricate meal, a thousand miles away, can't undo the years of suffering. So, this image will stay in my mind. Only I know how much I tried. The hurt will remain in my heart—the way you made me feel. The conversation will remind me that love can't be forced. Silence told me my feelings weren't valued. The anger and frustration I felt that night will remind me I made the right choice.

I was left sitting alone at the table, deserted once again. I never turned to watch him walk away. The sheer drapes swayed with the breeze, and the tears I hesitated to show fell quietly to the sound of the ocean. For a moment, I wished I had dined alone because I did deserve all this—a lovely candlelight dinner under the stars next to the ocean.

The Crown Jewel

I'm seated in a luxury jewelry store; the pieces of fine jewelry sit with me in tranquility waiting patiently for an owner. The stones sparkle, each setting off vibrant dazzles from the unnatural light that unknowingly lures in its prey. I've always taken my liking to fine jewelry over its cosmetic counterparts. But today, I have no interest. I sit here like a child that has been scolded and will be coaxed into whatever the parent chooses fit.

When did it come to this? When did I lose interest in all the things I loved? I was a different person then and now I feel alienated in my own body.

The sophisticated sales agent places a bottle of sparkling water in front of me. This is the difference in service you receive here as opposed to shopping in a mediocre boutique. You get unmatched service; they make you feel extra special but somehow it's not working today. Today this luxury brand is nothing but metal with a stamp on it. I watch the bubbles clustered together as they float to the top of my glass, pairing nicely with the diamonds secured in place beneath the glass showcase. I feel quite the same, trapped, like a bird in a cage with no hope of escape.

I watch the passersby. A couple arm in arm are window shopping. I watch their faces and wonder if they, too, are hiding behind some veil. Today, I would rather be on that side of this scene, merely desiring an ornament lavishly displayed in the window.

I was brought here and ushered into this shop that I adored, but now, I feel sickly looking at these items of bribery. One of them will go home with me today and any other woman would be ecstatic to receive such an extravagant gift, but me? I'm far from overjoyed. I feel helpless, waiting patiently to go back to whatever it was that robbed me of myself.

The piece of jewelry I'll take home today will remind me how I don't love the man who brought me here. I'll have no choice but to accept it. It will, however, become evidence that I indeed accepted this gesture of endearment. It will remind me this piece was a trade for love, a love that doesn't exist. What he fails to understand is he cannot buy my love or my happiness. He cannot buy my feelings and my heart; he also cannot buy back the pain that he has caused. It will become evidence that he supposedly tried to make this relationship work.

Nothing can make this crown jewel sparkle again. She has lost her shine and her zest for life and for love. He took her for granted and failed again to see her real worth.

Secrets

"Can you keep a secret?"

I looked up before I answered, confused at the statement but curious as to what was about to be said that needed an announcement in order to be revealed. "Sure, if you want me to," I answered.

I'll store it with the rest of them, because somewhere in the back of my mind, I have hundreds of collected secrets. They've accumulated over the decades. For the most part, they're just gathering dust.

I sometimes wonder why I was the chosen one. Perhaps I'm a good listener, I'm nonjudgmental, or I refrain from colliding with the crowds on the need to gossip. I'm unsure if I even remember them all, but my conscience doesn't allow me to repeat. Once in a while I'll pick an old one and use it as an example for a life lesson. I am in possession of small inconsequential secrets and then the shocking confidential ones that made me freeze in my skin. Years ago, I was moved by such information, but now nothing surprises me. I suppose with life experiences you learn that someone's secret is about their life, and they have a right to live it on their terms, secret or no secret.

I recall secrets I'm still holding on to for people who left my world or for those who couldn't do the same for me, but I still kept theirs. It's the secrets that let us down and then it's the secrets that save us too. Kind of ironic, isn't it? We all live with secrets, big and little incidents we'd rather not share; we'll take them with us when we leave, and no one will ever know. Some secrets, as in this occasion, we feel the need to disclose. Is a secret even a secret if it's shared? If you don't tell, does it become a lie? If you don't know, will it hurt? If it makes you happy, is it still wrong?

For the most part, secrets are withheld to not hurt others, but we hurt when we hold on to them. My secrets, the ones I kept to myself, ate away at me slowly. A few secrets I hesitantly disclosed left me feeling guilty. I confided and then wished I hadn't. Then there are secrets folks kept from me. The ones that, when finally released, deformed me, left scars, and I couldn't get past the truth. Eventually, you learn to reconcile and move on. They become life lessons.

Every person I know, in some way or form, is a tad dissatisfied. Either secretly wishing they lived a different life, or are living two, and the very few that are content now, have a speckled past of secrets. We all have an unpublished side. Even your soul mate doesn't know everything. You can't climb inside someone's head or heart; you'll never know entirely what they're thinking or feeling. And so, our thoughts also become secrets, our desires and fantasies become secrets of another kind.

There's an old proverb that says, "If you don't want anyone to find out, don't do it." Yet we do it anyway. It gives us a thrill or sense of satisfaction to hide our secret life. In some form we all live a double life. It's this second secret life that fulfills our inner thirst for a forbidden adventure. We venture out and do things we shouldn't or are ashamed of. Then perhaps it's our conscience that we can't live with that allows us to confide in another we trust, because keeping it inside will eventually torture us, but telling will help release from that burden. Maybe it's because we seek justification that in some strange way, it was a choice we had no choice but to choose.

And so, as I listened to another secret, I, too, began packing it away. "Do you think I'm a bad person?" I was asked. "No," I answered. "Secrets don't make you a bad person."

During the day, the universe will watch your every move, and when night falls, we all put our secrets to rest. We tuck away all those malignant pieces that we need not reveal. We make ourselves believe we're unimpeachable. In time, you, yourself, will realize if it was worth keeping or giving away your secret.

Silence

It was, at times, unbearable, like in the car, the tension of having to drive a distance with nothing to say. Talking became work, the thought of having to keep up a conversation like we were strangers with nothing in common, once again. I kept silent. My guidance wasn't welcome either when he'd take a wrong turn. I watched the volume dial get turned up, even if I had something to say, I was silenced. Looking out of the window, I watched the world go by, my silence followed behind. He controlled everything: the ride, the time, the music, and me.

I received no help making my way out of the car or being escorted inside the venue. Inside, we drifted apart as if we had pre-rehearsed the entire scene. I lost him in the crowd. Was I sad? No. It was liberation of sorts, gaining life for a few hours from the constraints of endless confinement. Was I disappointed? Yes. I did wish we were normal, like other couples. Arm in arm, drinking and laughing together, not on display, fearing when my freedom would end.

I never expected my life to be silenced, that one day I'd shut down completely. The silence that consumed me made me believe there was no hope for a better tomorrow. I became silent because fighting exhausted me; silence gave my eyes a break from the tears that became weary of crying. I'd stare at the pages of a book as if they were blank because I couldn't comprehend what was being scanned, and there was no motive in anything I did. Silence kills your will to try, and eventually, you just find yourself standing and staring into nothingness.

I consumed food because it was there. I drank to quench a thirst that I didn't know existed. I'd try hard to engage in conversations, but somewhere along the line, my mind would drift off, and I would see the lips move but not hear a word. I'd manage to smile at some humor that was expressed, but I didn't get the joke, and with that, I slowly retracted from the crowd. I had this false illusion that my family and friends were there to save me. I realized very quickly that no one could save me, and so I began a slow descent from the very things that had kept me going. I silenced my inner being.

Now and again, I'd see him faintly in the crowd; now and again, he'd appear to show me he was present. I watched his behavior toward others, how differently they were treated, how expressive and attentive he was, as if nothing was amiss in his life. What an act he put on, or was it? I commended him for his ability to show care and emotion to anyone but me. He could make me feel worthless at the click of a finger, throw at me the most hurtful comments, make me believe I was crazy, and then, as if the aftereffects of his thunder had no impact, he'd walk out. Just like a storm passes with no mercy, but the damage? It is left for the innocent to pick up. Why couldn't I be like him? Nothing fazed him; everything hurt me.

I listen as he speaks; he never stops, but has nothing relevant to say to me. I listen to his raised pitch, I feel the heat, and watch his anger. We lived most of our lives in a silence of sorts. That silence was different; we kept out of each other's way and just went about our lives. We talked to discuss matters at hand. This silence happened out of hurt; I became silent because I was failing. I tired myself of trying to put up a fight and trying to make something work that had no hope. What I didn't know was that silence is actually deadly. It was the silence that created the scene for an attack. It gave birth to a monster. It was the silence that caused damage to my character. It opened up wounds that I had put to rest. Purposely digging deeper and making me so sore I couldn't deal with the agony, so I chose to silence it.

How much poison can one take before it ends? I continued to drink and drink with no end in sight. We know and yet we say nothing. It's what is haunting me that will take my life, and what is killing me that can set me free. My world came crashing around me. I fought in silence, then wept in silence, and finally I gathered myself, waiting in silence for the next time.

I couldn't be the hero in his story, no matter how hard I tried. From within these very walls, a misogynist appeared, and I became its prey. Some things just don't work together. Exhaustion sets in, and hope says its final goodbye; It took my soul with it. From the constraints of not speaking, I become the villain in his performance. I did, however, learn one more thing: silence is also the best revenge.

PART III

Beauty Is in Acceptance

The art of self-expression, remaining unique and embracing change - beauty is not in perfection.

- My Identity Page 76
- The Tigress Page 79
- Serenity Page 81
- Pastime Page 83
- An Age-Old Love Affair Page 86
- Sunday Kind of Love Page 89
- Behind Every Successful Woman Page 91
- Timeless Beauty Page 94
- A Lady in Need Page 97
- Do You Feel It, Your Age? Page 100
- My Mother, the Bride Page 103
- I Know My Worth Page 106
- What Makes Me Strong? Page 109
- A Lust Story Page 112
- The Yogi Page 114

My Identity

I don't know who I am anymore," I whispered. I remember that crisp Autumn day like it was yesterday. I was offered a cup of hot tea to calm me. I continuously dunked the tea bag in the china cup to stop my fingers from trembling. I met with a holistic healer for therapy. I lifted my gaze from the teacup, looking at her curly hair, brown eyes, and fair skin. I asked, "Do you know the person you are? I mean, do you know who you really are on the inside?" I had confused myself with the statement I made. She tried her best to coach me, but I couldn't reveal to her who "me" was.

I didn't even know how to feel because I looked elsewhere for validation. I wore what was expected of me. I was talked over and hardly given a chance to express my opinion. I was expected to play certain roles, and those roles took away from my true identity. There is a difference between being yourself and being yourself to please another.

Every person has their own identity. Yet it's also true that you can lose it. I've been there, where you're stripped from the person you were meant to be. You don't even realize it's happening until one day, you wake up, and you've lost all control over yourself. Occasionally, I'd look at my reflection in the mirror, and I didn't even recognize myself. I was there in person, a person that someone else wanted me to be. I walked around with a filter, my thoughts remained in my head, and my conversations with myself were fitting for someone who was disconsolate. It's the trespassing that weakens you and the constant tampering that allows the insecurities to pile up. Identity is not only your physical presence; there is a mental and emotional aspect to it as well. It's who you are in your organic state, before the noise of your surroundings zones in on you.

I can't tell you my life wasn't fulfilling, of course it was. I accomplished a lot. But, I didn't know who I really was until much later in life. I didn't come to terms with myself as an individual until I had no choice but to work on myself. When there was no other person influencing my decisions or watching my every move, did I know the real "me"? I became oblivious to my own rights, and little by little, I gave up those rights to satisfy others. Liberation is the act of being set free from oppression. Victory happens when you win at something you were failing at. Facing something you were afraid of is liberation with victory. That is exactly how I gained back my identity. I would be lying if I told you it was easy.

And then somehow, they are different, but cannot express their true individuality because society speaks for us. The journey of learning who you really are, for some, is not an easy ride. They hide and please for the sake of not being singled out or not accepted. Why do they have to fit in? Why can't they belong with the rest? No one should need to be validated or meet expectations. Why should you conform to someone else's beliefs? We all do it. We stare, point, and judge. We do it because what is "normal" works for the majority, but when someone is out of place, we speculate. It doesn't fit into our realm of normalcy, and so we're not satisfied, because the reality is, it makes us uncomfortable.

I can only talk from experience; they tell me, as a human being, your first right is to own your identity. It's your right to live on your own terms and own a brand of your own. "Being you" shouldn't require another person's intrusion. You should be accepted for who you are, nothing more, nothing less. In a world where everything is copied, you should remain unique. Your identity is your passport through life, own it!

The Tigress

I hear the distant hustle and bustle of the city fading as we enter the animal kingdom, the birds chirping, and nothing but the engine sound of our jeep. It's a dirt road in the middle of a jungle, a natural reserve that is home to the majestic Indian tigers. The bumpy ride on this dirt path is anything but forgiving on my back. But I'm not at all worried; the excitement of even sitting in this jeep is no less of a dream, really.

Today, I get to check it off my bucket list: a wild safari. The dust is rising like smoke from the running tires, and my mouth becomes parched from the aftereffects. The smell of wildlife opens up what seems like your seventh sense, and I'm inhaling the smell of mystery and open wilderness and the animals that you only see in their natural habitat. I'm amazed by the vastness of this land, the mountains, the foliage, and the rock formations that hide stories of the small creatures and the majestic giants that walked their path.

The sun is setting, and through the haze appears the unmatched beauty that attracts many to explore this jungle. It's definitely mystifying. I'm accompanied by the driver and my guide. He looks very generic; his brown skin shows the many hours he spends under the sun driving around spectators. I'm most fascinated by my guide. She shares my mother's name, and she is as fierce as she was. Her knowledge of this forest and the animals that reside here is enthralling. I listen in awe as she explains how to spot a tiger's footprint and when it is fresh. She talks as if she lives amongst them, sharing habits and diet, and patterns that set them apart from other animals that share these very surroundings.

This woman, who resides in a village nearby, has small children and a house to feed, but her love for animals comes first. It's very noticeable, her love for these creatures. The difference here is, she actually wears a uniform and gets to do what she loves; she tells her stories of the reality of trekking hours in search of those wild ones. I'm intrigued by her stamina for the waiting game and her watchful eye, how she directs the driver to our target. She knows all the moves they're making and the ones they will make. Her appearance doesn't match her personality, but I'm proud that a woman is sitting beside me. I catch pictures of the wildlife, somewhat excited and a tad anxious as to what may approach next. We sat at times, silently, our eyes scanning the terrain and getting startled by every hustle of foliage.

We didn't get to see a tiger directly cross our path, just in the faint distance. We saw its prey, and it hurt my feelings, making me sick to look at it. A cow lay dead on its side, the predator's claw marks visible. "The tiger will be back," she says confidently. "It doesn't share prey with anyone, not even another tiger." She comforts me, telling me it is the cycle of life. I'm not one bit scared, and she commends me on my courage. She continues her stories of how the tigers invade the nearby villages occasionally, as if they are harmless cats. It doesn't trouble her one bit. "We are the ones that invaded their land, so they have every right."

As we head back, she apologizes for not being able to lure a tiger nearer. I tell her that just being here was an experience of a lifetime, and to have this tigress beside me made it worthwhile.

Serenity

Some of life's placid moments come when you are motionless, simply observing, and the mind is still. It is then that you acquire peace, and your surroundings have little effect on you. It's a thinking process for me; I bear no resemblance to a meditative mind. After a hectic few days and much travel, I'm ready for tranquility.

The ocean is lying still, almost morphed with the sky, making it hard to spot the fine line of the horizon. The sky and sea bear the same hue as aqua. In the distance, small islands sit still, like animals emerging from the great waters. This is how unreal this picturesque view unfolds in front of me.

My gaze follows colorful fishing boats way out in the gulf, and closer to the shore, I see the last of the jet skis and speedboats halting for the day. The tide brings with it swimmers and paddleboarders. It's almost dusk here; the faint breeze does no justice to the heat. This heat is different; it's scorching but somehow much needed for excreting that toxic buildup. This faint ocean breeze is helping the palm trees sway a little more now and again, to signal their presence here, towering above me.

The stout Thai masseuse is working wonders on my legs. Together with this view, it satisfies the notion that this could be a little bit of heaven on earth. She's releasing physical tension, but this view, too, is releasing emotional restlessness. The organic flute music plays rhythmically to the bounce of the small waves as they come to kiss the white sands and ripple away, giving chance to another set.

When my thoughts wander from this scene, I realize that while I am cleansing my mind and body, I am, in turn, burdening this woman. She will take home my exhausting energy today. As she kneads into my limbs, I feel myself releasing the tightness. She must obviously feel the tension because she repeatedly returns to the same spot finding it hard to detangle. She must encumber some of it. Whether it's positive or negative energy, she will, in turn, be attached. I wonder how she manages this task she's graciously taken on. This must leave her feeling drained at the end of each cycle. How does she do this every day and yet remain so calm and collected? I understand it is her chosen work; nothing comes easy. We all give up something to gain something. We all take on professions for the betterment of ourselves and some for the betterment of others; those are the fulfilling roles, the gratifying work that is done with compassion. I wonder if she enjoys her work. I'm guessing yes, as she hums, her hands glide and unleash the tightness.

I tell myself my mood shouldn't shift from the ritual of cleansing, so I am trying hard now to enjoy this little bit of paradise. I am blessed to have acquired. Her magical hands are doing wonders, and instead of quieting my mind and surrendering to the release, once again I find myself deep in thought. Another question, another subject to ponder upon while I relax.

Pastime

The deafening sound of the leaf blower seems tolerable after a few minutes; it somewhat disguises the street noise. It's hot and sticky today, and the fan towering above me isn't justifying its speed. I ordered a bottle of water and ice to go with it in hopes that it would not only quench my thirst but also alleviate my body temperature somewhat. I'm waiting patiently for company, and they're late. I'm also now wondering why I took outdoor seating in a garden setting, as I feel the droplets of sweat slide down my back.

I shoo away the pesky mosquitoes that always seem to be engrossed by leaving me bumpy lesions that last for days. The gardener doesn't seem one bit phased by the scorching heat or the bugs. I watch him go about his business, masking nobly under the beaming sun. I smile back, and he continues. He's an older gentleman. I wonder why he's taken on such a tedious task; he does it with admiration, like it's his own piece of land. You can see the lines of his life indented on his forehead, and his hands tell me they've rooted many plants. He seems in no rush to complete his work, and I like that he's leisurely and passionate. He fiddles with every leaf that seems astray and accurately measures the moisture in every pot with his worn hands. I reckon he's an accomplished gardener.

Unlike me, he doesn't reach for gloves as his hands muddle with the soil. A true mark of a farmer, no doubt. He wipes the remaining dirt on his overalls and wobbles to the next plant. At one time, it was hard for me to associate being orderly and polished with cultivating a garden. Then I became a gardener myself, and I realized perfection can be obtained with anything you set your mind to.

Suddenly, the noise from his machinery halts, and I'm back to hearing the swoosh of the traffic. I even notice the whimsical wind chime faintly clinking, and next to it, the bird feeder. His instruments must have frightened them away. I begin to slouch in the heat as my eyes follow his every move. He must be someone's granddad, I'm guessing. This must be his hobby to fill his spare time during the day. I wonder what his other profession was before he took up gardening.

We all need a pastime to make us feel good. A diversion of sorts, if you will. Some leisurely pursuits to offset the madness of our everyday haul. Our lives are contaminated with a list of "to-dos." We are in a constant switched-on mode, from school to college to work, juggling family, children, parents, and our social network. When we finally begin winding down, it doesn't come so easily.

We still look for things to occupy our minds. Part of me understands the need to keep busy; it keeps us from unnecessary thoughts. The other half resonates with enjoying the fruits of our labor. We work hard, so we deserve this time to relax. But the irony is, we are so used to being busy, a peaceful lifestyle is hard to get accustomed to. We all need a divertissement that requires no complex effort; something which we love to do, something we are good at. Something that takes us away from our troubles in life. We should find the time to do things that make us happy to be alive.

My gardener friend replaces the blaring sound of his leaf blower with a sweet humming and winks as he approaches me. We engage in conversation mainly about plants, and I get excited about sharing my own gardening experiences. I see the passion in his eyes, and I listen to his romance for the plants. He agrees, we all need a passion we can keep pursuing in life, it helps you stay young and vibrant. It helps with diluting some of the stress and cleanses the mind. Putting it simply, it should fulfill you and balance out your affairs of living life.

An Age-Old Love Affair

"We met in high school," the soft voice whispers to me as she puts her frail hand on my arm and draws me closer. The elderly couple I'm accompanying on my walk is an inspiration for me today. It was like a breath of fresh air to see two elderly people very much in love.

They fell in love some 80-plus years ago, in high school, and from what I can feel at this moment, it is the same love they gave birth to, so long ago. I watch as each one of them pauses to let the other finish off the sentence, and I'm in awe of the beauty of this relationship I'm getting to witness.

Into their 90s now, they both were very much alert and beautifully secure in their skins. It's inevitable that with age, one becomes weak and slow. There is also a huge blessing in living together this long. As they recited their stories to me, I felt as if we were worlds apart. I wasn't born when they started their journey; they lived through wars and revolutions, and through it all, they didn't let go of one another. They were both strong enough to walk their own walk, yet in some compelling way, they both held each other up with respect and kindness.

I could see the fondness with which they took care of each other; they both glowed in their own light. The deep lines on their faces were filled with rich history, and the silver hair so immaculately kept told a story of its own. Their indented smiles radiated warmth from having lived a deserving life. It was through their endearment and warmth that I saw a kind of gratification of life itself, one that had been worth living.

"We've been married seventy-six years," she continued, and for a split second, I felt like a failure. It was definitely an accomplishment to be celebrated. This was a definition of marriage, a ritual full of compromises, trust, and respect for each other; it is how it is held up. Throughout their journey, one of them must have waited for the other to catch up; they never allowed the other one to walk behind, just as they were doing now.

"We have children, but no grandchildren,", she said as she let go of my arm, and for a sudden moment, my heart skipped a beat, and then, as if she knew, she consoled me. I heard the sadness in her voice. "It is what it is." And as if it didn't matter, they moved on. I found it hard to grasp this statement. Oh, how life plays us! Here were two wonderful individuals who were missing an entire piece of their future lineage. If anyone deserved the blessing of grandchildren, it was them.

As we walked, I listened to their stories of yesteryears and the enthusiasm with which they were told. It's all we have in the end, the stories we want our loved ones to hear. They don't need anything at this point in their lives, just someone to listen. We made jokes and exchanged numbers, and I wish to continue our friendship not because they need a listener but because what I saw was something so delightful, yet rare.

As I bid them farewell, I became encompassed in my own pool of thoughts. How wonderful it must be to hold on this long to the love of your life. To have shared a lifetime and know you were never alone. To have that adoration for one another and be able to pull each other up and walk hand in hand. Yet to gain something, we all must lose too, and I felt it as they accepted this journey with no one to pass on their legacy. I was moved by this heavenly relationship, the beauty of their love, but it too had a flaw, a gentle reminder that nothing is perfect.

Sunday Kind of Love

Easy, relaxed, just like Sunday mornings, that's how love should be, nothing complicated, simply basic and comprehensible. When the lust of Saturday wears off, waking up to the trance of an easy Sunday love should see you through the uncertainty. Why make it a complex game of yours and mine when what's yours is yours and what's mine is mine? Let it be. Let the clarity sink in and the hesitation unfold.

Time doesn't exist on Sunday mornings; minutes morph into hours in between the endless ticking of time that has yet to be. This is Sunday morning love, right here in between the blankets, in between my thoughts, in between the end and beginning of another week. The pillow that cradles my head, the deep sigh that does nothing to alert me out of the comfort of my sheets… this Sunday morning, I want nothing but to feel solitude. When day breaks, I'll lie in the light that forced its way through the sheets and with each flutter of my eyelids I'll make a wish, that every Sunday morning feels just like this.

Sunday mornings feel like the coffee smothered in steamy foam. Like the warmth of a summer sun on your face, the same way water glides off your skin. Just like the breeze that ever so slightly caresses your hair, Sunday mornings should be easy-breezy effortless. Don't tell yourself you're being negligent and you are not worthy; the world will wait. Sunday mornings are to be cherished, to be lazy and unwilling to use an ounce of energy that may otherwise be wasted on mindless chores.

Sunday mornings speak to me of how my imperfections became perfect and how the sound of my flaws was music to someone's ears. How I caught every breath that needed an escape, and how the sweet scent of something wanted was inhaled slowly. My being is not compromised; it is me, shielded in my own cocoon. I bask in the safe space, holding on to the moment when nothing more matters. Grasp a little longer to the warmth and the beats that rhythmically tell a tale of two hearts. I'm spooned in skin and the embrace of a heavy hand. I'd touch the softness and glide along the crevices. If I were to let go, I'd fall apart, and who doesn't want to be wrapped in a secure blanket of affection, to be held together.

There's nothing to speak of, no agenda to be discussed, just enveloped in silence and embraced in desire. It's an affair, not from the lust of Saturday night, but an affair of yearning to be loved like Sunday morning. These mornings were not made for thinking or talking; just to rest and dwell. These mornings are made for uncomplicated pleasures. A kind of love made just for Sunday mornings.

Behind Every Successful Woman

To me, a successful person is one who has mastered many attributes in one's lifetime. Riches alone do not make you successful. Your qualities and traits, together with your ability to have compassion and respect, earn your distinction.

I used to believe that behind every successful person there was a support system. I was superficially led to believe a family would stand beside you through thick or thin. They would support you, but that was an infatuation, for me anyway. I belong to Gen X. We are sandwiched in between the baby boomers and the millennials, the bridge between the older and younger generations. The women of my generation did a lot of supporting. We delivered, and most times it was a thankless job. The saying, "Behind every successful man is a woman," is valid; I did prove that right in my lifetime. The successful men in my life had me backing them up.

I was never reluctant to support, aid, or otherwise bear the load. I never second-guessed a hand in need. Contributing my efforts enabled me to feel essential, and that need was my ticket to give more. I gave more in the affair called marriage, too. When you bear equal weight, you're demonstrating success bifold. Bearing more than you can handle leaves you debilitated. Watching yourself deteriorate, trying to bear an uneven load, is when the disconnect begins. I was looking for support, even a gesture of recognition was enough, and most of my life, that simple act went unappreciated. I carried on bearing the load. It's disheartening, and eventually the inevitable happens, and you not only disengage, but you're also sapped of whatever energy you had, and then you become paralyzed.

Running a home, raising children, caring for elderly parents is not really considered work or even success for that matter. Making a living, which I did equally, was the fruit that showed the appeal for my success. I was also made to believe that I wouldn't make it out there alone. My dependency on a man was a predetermined fate. I couldn't succeed without a successful man backing me up. Quite sad when you think about it. We have made our way into the 21st century, yet such outdated beliefs still lurk around. My definition of feminism has nothing to do with gender equality, because we can never be equal. How can we be? We need balance in any relationship, a person who can bear the load equally.

Someone once told me I wasn't made for a job I had undertaken. I managed a smile as he gave me his unwanted opinion. The short one-sided conversation made me ponder his idiotic arrogance. I questioned his morals, and did I intimidate him? There is a separation between such individuals; the variance is in mindset. You feel superior, but I am modest. You're patronizing, and I'm humble. You can think you're smarter because you are louder. You feel the need to be heard, and I don't feel the need to engage. You seek attention, and I have no interest in being noticed. I am resilient, both physically and mentally, and I am enough. There are opponents out there who are intimidated by the confidence I've mastered. They should be; my success came with a price, and it's in the qualities I possess. Why is it so hard to digest a simple fact?

Sadly, and this may surprise a few too many, I walked behind a man, but he was never behind my success. There was never a man cheering me on. Yet here I am—I built, I raised, I gave, I supported,

I endured. There was never a "me" that stood by me. I did it alone, and I'm still doing it alone.

"Behind every successful woman is herself." ~ Halle Berry

Timeless Beauty

While on my travels, I had the privilege to converse with a gentleman. He was a journalist and a publisher, and he traveled the world. The afternoon we met, we had a very meaningful conversation. It turned out we had a lot in common; we shared the same birthday, and we both enjoyed writing, wine, and cheese. He was quite a bit older than me and you could tell he had lived an interesting life. His mature features conveyed good judgment about the wisdom he shared, and his mannerisms told me he was accustomed to many different cultures.

As we pondered over bubbly and bites, I noticed what set him apart was his doddery ability to get the attention of passersby and his eccentric politeness. He was definitely distinctive. During our interaction, his quirkiness humored me; for instance, he carried his spice shaker for his meals. He spoke many dialects, and this also intrigued me. He was unique and very proud of himself and his accomplishments, a well-grounded gentleman.

As we discussed life, he proceeded to give me lessons on aging. He asked me what I thought was the most beautiful thing about myself. I sat silently for a few moments because I had never thought about it, let alone had an answer waiting to be disbursed. I answered with a question: "Maybe my smile?" He laughed as his deeply embedded wrinkles showed how much I humored him. "That is what the audience finds beautiful about you, dear, but what do you think is beautiful about yourself?" I couldn't come up with an answer, but I told him I'd think about it more and get back to him. While I was disoriented, he was still amused.

I told him, I found myself disproportionate for lack of trying to find a better word to fit my middle-aged figure. Although I would have otherwise been offended by anyone agreeing, he did agree. But he said that had nothing to do with the question at hand. He continued to tell me the great love of his life was Sophia Loren, and she was disproportionate, but she was also an image of timeless beauty. The Roman Empress captured many hearts. I myself once idolized her. When I thought long and hard, I began to realize he was right; she wasn't at all perfect, much rather the opposite. It was the way she carried herself, the way she spoke, and her mannerisms that made her the most attractive. She was beautiful in her own way.

The original question continued to bother me. How is it that I don't know what is beautiful about myself? I'm at the peak of my life, and I don't know what I find beautiful about myself. Do we maneuver into phases of our lives, and fix things we see in the mirror as faults, and not notice the real beauty we hold? Why are we trying so hard to look a certain way and fit a certain mold? Why are we pleasing others, and what are we gaining from it all? The biggest question being, why are we not in tune with the beauty within?

As I bid farewell to my newfound friend, I continued recalling the advice and thoughts of this man, who in one sitting, taught me about being beautifully confident in my own skin, to allow myself to love myself. It didn't matter that I was just starting in midlife. My past didn't matter to him; my age didn't matter at all. It had no relevance that I was starting over and had just begun writing. What mattered was the way I spoke about myself. "Speak of your accomplishments with pride," he said. "Not about what destroyed you but what made you." He told me to give myself the time to learn about my true self, the gift of believing in myself, and knowing that nothing is more important. "Don't speak ill of yourself," he told me. "Believe you are beautiful." His words impacted me, and I realized that no matter what your faults are or what has blemished your soul, always remain positive, original, and true to yourself. How we perceive ourselves is a reflection of maturity and our belief in ourselves. Not knowing about ourselves is a reflection of insecurity, and a skeptical attitude is doubting oneself.

I began to dissect little by little the things I liked about myself. This exercise allowed me to free myself of any shallow esteem lurking within me. I began to accept my flaws and began to show off my positive qualities. I gained more confidence on a distinct level.

How I carry the load of my life, how I display my character, and how maturely I frame my figure, all bring together the person I am. My beauty isn't just surface level, but rather skin deep. I'm aware of my mannerisms, my speech, and my attitude towards another human being. It's all part of what makes me attractive. In the end, he did agree. "Your smile is beautiful, dear, and you carry this attractive quality very well. The grace in which you carry yourself makes you the most unique and appealing, but you have yet to answer the question for yourself..."

A Lady in Need

An arm reached out from behind me and opened the door. I must admit, I was taken aback. I couldn't remember the last time a gentleman opened a car door for me. Jokingly, I said, "You're on the wrong side!" A little humor never hurt anyone, but this humor hid the truth about the actual feelings that gave birth at that moment.

I almost felt as important as the luxury vehicle I was about to step into. Was it an infatuation in my head that allowed me to believe I was actually worth this kind of treatment? It was the feminism in me that led me to believe I didn't need this nonsense from a man, and now it suddenly became the old-fashioned lass in me that desired an obsession to be treated like a lady.

There were gentle signs of adoration that floated around the table. It was the attentiveness to my conversation that allowed me to talk freely. It was the hand across my waist that guided me to my seat. It was the words of encouragement that allowed me to choose what I desired on the menu. Above all, it was the hours that passed in a moment because I was made to feel valued.

Everyone on this earth has a need buried deep down, a need for want, acceptance, or simply to be desired. We also fear rejection on certain levels. We're very good at putting up a false face or making ourselves believe we don't want something when we know we can't have it. It makes it easier to deal with, a false sense of satisfaction.

It's our needs that sometimes prevent us from enjoying the very things we have already acquired. It's also our needs that tell us our desires are unfulfilled. I would be foolish to say that fulfilling our needs is not important. For instance, we humans are a tactile species. Each one of us desires touch to some extent. Even those who keep to themselves are the ones who need to touch the most because they're fighting with some deep emotions. Battling demons of resentment towards past bitterness. We put up our guards, but it doesn't discount the fact that we still long for affection.

There is nothing wrong with wants and needs, but there is something very wrong with believing that we are not worthy of kindness, regard, or attentiveness. It's very easy to suppress a desire for fear of rejection or even have the ability to think it's unattainable.

Throughout my lifetime, my expectations diminished. I became comfortable with mistreatment, and eventually, I realized a part of me was expecting too much. We all expect to some extent. If I am expecting to be treated a certain way, I too must push the same behavior, but it tires you when you keep giving and receiving nothing in return. The irony of this massacre unraveled itself when I realized I had no idea how to behave in the presence of all this gentility. It caught me off guard, and I wasn't sure how to accept the gestures. I opened my own car doors, pulled up my own chair, someone talked over me always, ordered for me, and left me at the table alone because their manners didn't follow them. You can't miss something you never had, but along the same line, you process the thought of having it anyway.

This particular event also surfaced shameful truths. How can a car be valued more than a human? How can luxury materials be treated with so much care, and yet a person be degraded to the point of feeling worthless? I suppose I forgot what it was like to be treated like a lady. It was a simple encounter, going out for a meal, that perhaps enlightened my perception of how I would like to be treated. It became an observation for me on the fondness I had for being respected. Your company unveils the comfort with which you can communicate. I was willing to reveal a lot more because of the sentiments that were thrown at me. I realized I was craving a demeanor of a somber kind, one that left me feeling valued. Above all this, it is I who divulged deep down in my subconscious to that dormant underlying self-awareness, that had surfaced feelings of truly wanting to be treated like a lady respectfully, and now I want nothing less.

Do You Feel It, Your Age?

Birthdays are a commemoration of the beginning of something new, the anniversary of your birth. We celebrate the milestones so happily when we're young, until slowly they morph into just another day that passes by, and we aren't so eager anymore. It is very much a privilege to mature. No one wants to admit they know that each year, we in fact, lose a year of our lives. We're one year closer to the inevitable. We take life for granted until we lose someone who didn't deserve to go. It seems only then, for a short while, we look deeper within. We begin to contemplate our own lives.

Every year, as your birthday arrives, one must exercise a process. One in which you can have an insight into the depth of what makes up your existence and see where you're headed. We all need to backtrack into our lives and pull out our accomplishments, look deeper into our journey, the wisdom we gained, and the mistakes that changed us. We all need to study ourselves. Instead of reading someone else's book, write your own.

The way our life pans out is really in our own hands. We don't understand this simple concept until we get older. We have only ourselves to blame for the outcomes. So, when you suddenly feel older than you are, look within and figure out why. What's bringing you down or holding you back from living? Life is a rollercoaster ride; we're competing with the very time that is on our side. It's much later in life that we actually figure it out, and some of us never will. Every stage of our life teaches us what we need to learn, because we refuse to learn it any other way. We have to live it.

There was a time when I felt I was closer to the end than I wanted to be. That phase in your life where you can't handle it anymore. The burdens become heavier and your limbs frail. You realize you still have a while to go, but you simply can't. Life becomes an endless game, and you question and bargain with fate. The truth is, most of what I had experienced in life was not even living. Somehow, I had discounted my own life and made everyone else's a priority. I rarely lived in the moment, and I don't think I really knew how to. My existence was just that, existing. I kept myself busy, so busy that I didn't have time for myself. Life just passed by, and not for a moment did I stop to inhale the real beauty of it. My younger days were spent worrying about things not in my control. The bird's-eye view of my lifetime tells me I have come full circle, and now time is on my side. I stand here looking back at the very person who achieved so much yet lived so little and has so much more to experience. All of a sudden, I'm a different person racing with the same time.

It's the aged who acquired the knowledge and wisdom I sought when I lived in my youth. Then, as if by magic, I found myself right here, older and wiser. Had I gathered all the wisdom back then, I'd be a different person now. These days, age really does seem just a number to me. I know my youthfulness has an exuberance now that somewhat intimidates many. I allow only positive vibes into my space, and this zest for living has become a blessing. I cherish my days, I tell myself I deserve this, and I settle with it. I used to think my father was selfish; he almost always pleased himself. Today, as I drift through midlife, I find the need to be a little selfish. I deserve the position I give myself. I feel youthful because I love my life, I make time, I laugh a little more, I love waking up, and I love falling asleep. I enjoy my work and the ones who allowed me into their lives; I love them too. It's a simple solution, really.

So, I'd tell you too, to dig a little deeper into those nooks and crannies and pull those strings that need to be cut or restrung. Filter out the unwanted noise. Rearrange your priorities and fulfill your desires. Take a break from the race and really smell the roses. You must learn to choose wisely and walk your own path into the future, with an open mind and a longing to explore and experience all that life has to offer. End your story with the best chapters. Only then does the number become just a number.

So, do you feel it? Your age?

My Mother, the Bride

She wore red on her wedding day. Although the pictures that captured the event were all taken in black and white, you could visualize the color. Her lovely hazel eyes were not reflected as she shied from making eye contact with the lens. The pictures seized her simplicity, her innocence, and her shyness. I'm certain that is why my father must have chosen her. But in those photographs, the color is missing.

She's covered in the same deep pink that was chosen for my wedding. On her final day, I must admit, she looked more beautiful than I, on my wedding day. As she lay there, still and composed, I saw how her timidness had vanished, how life must have made her the woman she became, strong and fearless, but not strong enough. Her young porcelain face glowed against the rich lip color that matched her outfit, and she looked as graceful as ever.

Shades of red are the colors for an Indian bride, a representation of feminine strength that is portrayed in a Hindu deity. My mother was my representation of both beauty and strength.

When a married Indian woman dies before her husband, she is dressed like a bride on her final day. According to Hindu belief, life doesn't stop with one's death. The soul lives on and passes through cycles of reincarnation. And so, one is prepared for the life to come. A married woman is considered fortunate if her husband outlives her. No one is fortunate here, not him, not her, nor I.

My eyes didn't shift from your face. I have no recollection of any other human from the hundreds that were paying their respects that day. You slumbered as if at any moment you would awaken. I would break free from the ones that were holding me back and hug you as tightly as I could and tell you that I was sorry. Whatever happened, how it happened, I would take the blame.

The mantras that were being chanted on repeat echoed down to my soul. They are meant to bring peace to the departed, but they did just the opposite for me. My head pounded, and the confusion of it all saturated me. Over again, I asked the same questions: Why? How am I here? Why am I seeing you this way?

I touched your face to make sure you were still you. The coldness told me you were no longer with me; you never stirred, and so they let you lead, and I followed behind. We were all lost in sorrow. Losing you was the hardest thing I had dealt with in my life. There is something to be said for the eldest child. The bond of your firstborn, I spent the most time with you; this mother-daughter connection will also last until eternity. I may not hold your hand again, but my heart will hold on forever and ever.

You were dressed for a wedding that day, and yet you were going to a place where I would no longer have access to your smile, your comforting words, and your warm embrace. There was a congregation, a priest, and flowers, just like you must have had on your wedding day. We will see you off, except there will be no celebration, no photographs, no song and dance, as you would have enjoyed. You will be ushered from this world quietly.

Just like your wedding day, tears were shed, but now, not one was a happy one. These tears won't stop, and each time I remember you, they continue to fall. Even after years go by and I am still here, I will glance at your photograph and see your smile and watch how your motherly face never got a chance to age. I remember your traits because I now display your sarcasm and your heroism, and I, too, smile just like you.

I will tell your grandchildren all about you and how it is unfair that you left so young, and they missed the most beautiful being I ever knew. I will tell them how their young grandmother was a bride twice and what a beautiful bride you made on your last day.

I Know My Worth

Time only tells what you leave behind; it shows you how far you have come and how much effort it took for you to accomplish your goals. Time doesn't stand still for you; it's a race against it. Forever and ever doesn't exist; our time here is limited every which way you look at it. I do feel sorry for the arrogant person who thinks he's immortal. The ones who believe the world revolves around them.

I'm not here to negotiate my value with anyone; I know my worth. You don't always get what you want, but I'm not settling. I'm working on things no one can take away from me: my mindset, my character, my peace, and dignity. I no longer feel the need to be included, understood, or accepted. I've learned, whatever isn't making me happy or is disturbing my peace, whatever it is, whoever it is, doesn't deserve my time.

Every dream contains a reality; the sooner you get clued in to reality, the better off you'll be. There's a reason I don't walk with the crowd. I feel safer alone. I enjoy my own company, so you will have to compete with that. I don't just say I love you to hear it back, I say it, so you know where I stand. Yes, I overthink, but I'm also the one who overloves. I know manipulation can feel a lot like love. So, if you choose to love me, love me for the mad, insecure, messed-up person I am, not who you want me to be. I'm an acquired taste; I'm not everyone's cup of tea, but I'm not here to please everyone. Don't call me perfect; a lie is never a compliment. Don't make promises either. Promises are meant to be broken. I need your word. I don't warrant the need to control another person. I have no interest in dictating.

Bodies meet all the time; I want a union of the souls and mind. You have to be able to awaken the Sapio in me. I'm not easily flattered, and your luxuries don't interest me. I'm a simple person, seeking simple qualities. I'm here to be appreciated while I'm alive, so don't bring me flowers when I'm dead. I deserve them now, just like kind words. If you have nothing good to say to me, just don't speak. I have no energy for arguments; I can kill you with silence. Your degrees and successes do little for me if you lack respect. I don't need to be told I'm beautiful. I'm an heir to a lineage of beautiful souls, and I seek validation from no one. I have my own style, so I dress only for myself. It's a dreadfully elusive behavior to think money can buy you class, morals, and common sense. I've mastered the art of surviving. I've grasped confidence, and if that too intimidates you, you should move on.

If you can, accept me at my worst, at my best, and as I am. I'm here to learn from you, about you, about me, through you. I want someone who will ask me randomly what I'm doing, someone who knows what I'm thinking. I want that person to crave my vibe, vibe with my song. I want a matching twisted mind. I seek the soul with an infatuation for my impracticalities. I want someone who will cook for me because I know how to appreciate a good meal. Someone who isn't afraid to drink out of the same glass. I want to be with someone who finds me attractive at 10 p.m. when I've exhausted myself, I've washed off the day, and I'm in my natural state of insanity. I wear my smile the best, so I want someone who will never take it off.

Everyone comes with broken pieces. I want someone who isn't afraid of me. I'm a disturbed soul; I need to keep busy, so if you can calm me, you've tapped into a part of my untamed consciousness. I want someone who knows, just knows me, like when I need to be held, because a hug will heal me more than words. I want to be with someone who can just lie with me and listen when I make no sense. Someone who doesn't need to reply, just to understand. I also want my undisturbed space. I don't need your explanations, because if you have to explain, it's already too late; I'm not interested. I listen more than I talk, and I observe more than you know.

We all get over things, eventually. I don't want to be in it to get over it. There is nothing worse than meeting the right person at the wrong time. Nothing more hopeless than knowing you could have been magic together. Nothing worse than contemplating what could have been. I don't live with regrets, but from time to time, I do ask myself if I should settle, but then there is nothing worse than not knowing your own worth.

What Makes Me Strong?

The picture I used for this story is a poster that hung in my office for decades. I admired it with pride. I wanted to be that woman. Back then, I was young, and I wasn't quite sure what attracted me to it. It was said to be a masterpiece in advertising, and an unnamed woman is used as "saving humanity from conformity." When I looked at it each morning, it defined the substance of what womanhood meant to me, but somehow, something I lacked. It portrayed a woman who runs from the norm to break down barriers; she possessed both a strength and a weakness.

Recently, I was speaking to a friend about life. In a short while, we have become good friends. Our stories are different, our cultures are unlike, and our upbringings are also mismatched. We live at opposite ends of the world, yet unlike me, she is the epitome of intellect. Yet, some aspects of our lives as women remain identical. The journey of womanhood is a manuscript directed by the entire human race, no matter where we reside. Some of us walk in line with what is expected from us, and others choose to wander. We each have walked both these paths.

I am the eldest of us, and she admires me. What is it she sees in me that is so empowering? She tells me I am strong. With age comes wisdom, but also with age comes experiences, loss, harsh lessons, and some form of regret. Standing your ground for something you believe is empowering, but I never thought of myself as strong, much rather the opposite. The dictionary defines the word "strong" as being able to withstand great force or pressure, to be able to endure, and to be resilient. I suppose I have been resilient in my life. I became tough when I had no choice. My confidence and independence did, in fact, emerge from this strength. I walked a lonely path, and loneliness makes you tough. Strong is an intense word, and strength is something we all possess. At times, it emerges when we are at our weakest point, and other times, one loses the will to even try to find it.

Eventually, I chose myself over everything. I left behind things I know that many women wouldn't leave. I had to withstand the war and tolerate an unpleasant outcome. A life that was not serving me. I let it all go. At the time, I didn't feel strong; I felt like the weakest person on earth, a person that was not made for this battle. No one taught me to fight. No one could save me either. I had to learn how to be a warrior on my own. Strong means to face your demons, whether they are living in your head or in human form. It means to break the mold of silence, suppression, and depressive thoughts. Strong means to take another step even when you don't have anything left inside of you to fight. I battled many ailments this way. I found the will to keep going.

I tell girls I mentor that no one is born this way; life makes you resilient. I wasn't made for this, but life didn't give me a choice. It's not the strength that scares the race; it's the confidence that materializes from that durability. Not needing another person to fulfill your existence or to fight your battle for you does require a form of strength. Unfortunately, it is also a trait that hurts egos. I want to tell girls out there to embrace their womanhood, to consider it a privilege to be born as a woman. Only a woman can give birth to her own strengths. To use your feminine strength to become a warrior. Make your mark and break down the stigma. Change happens when you decide to walk off the beaten path. There will always be a disagreeable force that will pull you down. You have to learn to rise above that and conquer your dream. I have been heard by the young and learned from them, and I have been loved by the old and respected them. Every soul taught me something.

I, too, admire my friend for all the ways she is so different from me, in all the ways she has also broken the mold and walked her own journey. She has fixed her own crown and continued walking with her head held high, and for that I commend her. I realized my friend wasn't judging me for the decisions I made. She was admiring the form in which I maneuvered through my life. Endurance and determination have been the central traits of my survival. I didn't make mistakes in my life; I accepted them as lessons, and more importantly, I have no regrets. My advice or life experiences aren't meant for critiquing, nor am I here to preach. I am a woman who believes that we can all learn from each other and be role models. Life also taught me it's not rivalry that wins but empathy.

This same poster now hangs in my son's office. I felt a sense of acknowledgement and pride that he, too, embraced something I left behind. And if he hung it because it reminded him of his mother, then it, too, must remind him of the woman his mother has become, and I was that positive example of strength for him, too.

A Lust Story

It wasn't until I became a mature moon child that I found the hidden secrets of my sensuality. Had I not left another world, I would never have ventured out on a mission to find myself. I was tantalized by the thought of glimpsing into a vision of me that didn't previously exist but could.

The concoction was made up of ingredients I had disregarded in my past. Yes, I had briefly scanned such visuals and even read passages that aroused the womanness in me. Yet now, I was brewing an entirely different potion made up of intense spiritual, mental, and physical passion. I began humoring myself. I was looking in the mirror at an entirely different version of this female figurine.

I was skeptical because a woman of my age rarely fits the mold I was having no issues positioning myself into. In this phase, most women become oppressed or despondent. I, on the other hand, felt I was submerging into some tantric energy. My body isn't a perfect masterpiece, but for the first time in my life, I found myself accentuating my curves, becoming desirably sensual, or should I say, I could make myself feel that way. I maneuvered into sultry seduction, the same way perhaps lust begins.

I imagined myself craving and wanting to enjoy the art of intimacy. This time, the dynamics were different; I became easily aroused, and for whatever reason, I was hungry for an indecent proposal. I kept telling myself this risqué behavior was obscene and a respectable woman of my age doesn't allow herself to be lured into indelicate situations. But when one's mind and body reach a certain age, the need to be fearless overrides the desire to be decent. It is then that you acquire an adequate amount of nerve to pry into an adventure that should have taken place a long time ago.

I questioned even my loving consumption of aphrodisiacs, and yet they were never forbidden fruits. Perhaps they were now beginning to finally work. I had an appetite for passion, and so I explored.

Being alone gives you the freedom to wander into unknown territory, and for me, it was a subject I hadn't explored. In my previous life, I was never asked, just shown; I was never the initiator, and so I was never suggestive. I had shied from it and at times settled with the fact that it was something that just had to be done. Pleasure was hardly in the equation. I never led and never demanded. Now something had changed, and I had changed.

It's the timing in my life that opened up this door of passion. I came from a lineage of women who spoke little on this subject. My predecessors were ornate decorations, orchestrated but veiled. I'm flamboyant and alluring. Perhaps I'm the first to convey that my physique was meant for more than pleasing, I wanted to be pleased. Physical intimacy became a desirable sport. But this need in me would only be led with some chemistry; something would have to arouse the lioness within to satisfy her hunger. The Sapio in me would have to lead the way to a physical bond, one that gives birth only when two souls connect deeply.

I craved something that had never come easily for me, an unusual awakening of my sexual spirituality, and so I became an unchaste woman of mysterious seduction and much passion.

The Yogi

I look up at the second set of stairs and let out a big sigh. This small building has a lot of potential, but instead, it's sitting isolated in the midst of a campus. I picture a welcoming studio filled with a relaxing ambience, music, and scents that will aid in comforting one's mind. As I approach the top floor of the great room, I'm greeted by my spiritual coach, who, for the last few days, has tried to get me to meditate.

He opens up the windows to let in the sound of nature and asks me to lie down on my yoga mat. I see the sound bowls behind him, and they amuse me as much as his ability to make me feel comfortable. He has not been so successful in helping to quieten my mind, and in his willful little way, he has been determined to win this battle. Every day, a new set of apparatuses, chants, or lectures awaits me.

I ask him why this place is sterile and unkept; maybe if it were more welcoming, I could do better. He laughs and tells me that I don't need all that to settle my mind into meditation. "Nothing outside should affect what's going on inside," he tells me. I beg to differ, but reluctantly I agree and settle down.

I took this journey to a retreat to work on myself. I traveled to the birth country of yoga and Ayurveda. I suppose I was always a simple yet spiritual person, and then while healing from physical trauma quite some decades ago, I turned to yoga. In the beginning, I researched and self-taught and found my avenue for a therapeutic cure. I then went as far as yoga teacher training, but another physical blow stopped that dream in its tracks. But I never gave up on the practice.

In fact, yoga is not a practice; it is a way of life. It taught me to listen to my body. Yoga heals in ways we all need to learn. Stretching, sitting, and even the mere act of breathing are also work. Mindful work that takes effort when done correctly.

Yoga, to me, is discipline. It's being able to make the mind and body connection in harmony with your breath. In everything you do and in everything you set out to do, there is an element of conjunction with the mind and body. So many of us are misled into thinking that yoga means intricate poses and asanas that only the skilled can perform. When in fact, it's not that at all. Yoga means listening to your body, doing what is comfortable, and pushing a little more to strengthen and make amends with your limbs. It's unwinding, deeply connecting, and taking the time to have awareness of what is good and bad for your body. It helps you align with your spiritual self and the world beyond you. I've learned many things on this journey, and on this particular occasion, I learned something new.

As I lay there on the mat listening to the sound of the wooden stick softly making sounds with the bowl, my mind again wandered off into another dimension. I tried hard, as with the previous lessons, to try and bring it back to being present, but I failed. Practice, they say, makes perfect, but this practice never availed.

I felt like a child eager to go home from school as I sat up. I told him I thought I did pretty well this time, and he laughed. "I know you were not present, but tell me, what brings you peace, cleanses your mind, releases you, and helps you settle down?"

His concerned words warranted a serious answer. I took a moment as I lowered my gaze. "When I write," I said.

On this trip, I learned that meditation doesn't mean to sit for hours and chant mantras or have some sort of out-of-body experience, like I thought. Meditation is a mental exercise; it means to engage in the act of reflection. To have mental clarity and a calm state. And so, on this journey of self-awareness, I was taught that if my writing makes me feel these things, it was my source of meditation, and I should continue down that path.

"Everyone is different. There is no 'one size fits all' when it comes to your mental wellbeing. You have to do what works for you. The key is to be consistent," he advised. With these words, I took my leave. I looked around at the neglected building one last time. Perhaps it's not neglected; it just needs to find a way to be restored. I was happy that after much searching in many places, the yogi in me finally found her meditative space.

PART IV

Moving Forward

Growth, resilience, letting go, new beginnings - letting go is never easy, but in release we often find peace.

- YOLO Page 118
- Smoke Signals Page 120
- Forgiveness Page 123
- The White Pigeon Page 125
- The Ring Page 127
- Little Christmas Tree Page 130
- How to Unlove Page 134
- In Control Page 136
- Distance Makes the Heart Grow Fonder Page 139
- Worth a Celebration Page 141
- I Believe Page 144
- Don't Look Back Page146
- An Arranged Marriage Page 148
- My Father's Diary Page 152
- Reflect Page 155

YOLO

I pay for my ticket turnaround and say goodbye to my tour guide, for the time being. Once again, I ask if he would change his mind and accompany me, but he bows respectfully, declining my offer.

I smile and follow the signs to the cable car. It is a very warm day, mid-afternoon, and I'm in the middle of nature in all its splendor. Mountains of foliage surround me, and I walk carefully down a cobbled path. I pass signs in broken English and whimsical ornaments that amuse me. The people here did a wonderful job of maintaining the natural beauty of the island and preserving the landscape. After some time, I reached the small station for the cable car, which looked like a small, primitive bus stop. I look up at the steep mountain and begin wondering if this was a good idea.

I ring a bell as directed by a sign and wait. During the few minutes of peace, I hear the sweetness of nature, and I cannot fathom that I ventured to explore another nation and culture entirely alone. I feel liberated, almost as if I conquered a feat of sorts. The noise of machinery distracts me from my thoughts as an open carriage chains its way down the mountain to me. I'm greeted by the cable-car guy. I get seated, and the trek uphill begins.

The surrounding hills are basking in tropical plants, and I see small houses amongst them. In front of me, I'm greeted with a deep blue sky filled with fluffy clouds, and beneath them lies the ocean in all its glory. I am all too familiar with the sea, but today I get to set my eyes on a different version of it. The ride is an amazing experience. Every few feet, the view changes, and with every change, I'm in awe.

I exit the cable car and walk amongst a stone walkway that leads me even higher. By now, I feel like I have indeed reached the clouds. I follow the path to a huge treehouse-like structure nestled within the lushness. Climbing more steps to the top, I engage with the most breathtaking view. I enter a charming, quaint cafe, small and airy. I'm seated at a table in front of the magnificent view. I cannot believe I made it up so high. I look around, trying to take in everything that my eyes see.

As I sip on my coffee, the first sign I set my eyes on reads "YOLO." I laughed to myself because it should have read "SOLO," since I'm here alone. Underneath it in small letters reads, "You only live once." I stare at it for a moment, as if the joke I just made wasn't at all funny. Yes, you do only live once, and once is all you need if you know why your life is worth living. I came here, so far away from home, to walk off the beaten path, do something I never did before, find myself, see if I would make it alone, and to meet new people and explore a different part of the world. This breathtaking view showed me how a beautiful simple experience can rock your existence.

Why shouldn't you embrace spontaneity, take that chance, be a little impulsive? We create our own happiness. Make the most of the time you have here and let yourself go a little. We think too much, and too much thinking exhausts the mind. There is so much more to life than what we perceive. We all have a purpose, we are all capable, and we all have a life. I gained a little knowledge with this experience, and what I gained the most was the fact that I am capable of making it alone. Tomorrow was never promised to any of us, so seize the day and live to the fullest, because you do only live once and once is all you need, if you know how!

Smoke Signals

I blew into the icy air, and my warm breath made smoke signals. I could make shapes; it was fun until my dad lightly scolded me that it wasn't ladylike to pretend to smoke, which I didn't understand because my aunt smoked all the time. I wasn't pretending to smoke; I was good at making shapes in the air. Just like I was great at blowing the biggest bubbles with my gum. Nevertheless, he told me to behave responsibly because customers were approaching.

My finger tips, which protruded from my woollen gloves, had turned a shade of purple with the cold, but instead of warming them in my pockets. I continued handing packets to my dad from the box. The market was waking up, and my dad was displaying his merchandise with pride. Our stall wasn't big, and I don't know how much money it brought in, but his Saturday morning little side job kept us busy.

I learned from my dad everything I needed to know about money, savings, banking, insurance, and above all, being frugal. I questioned him and he taught me. That is how the entire process of entrepreneurship intrigued me. It was then, as a little girl, that I began dreaming of owning my own business. I didn't know what or how; all I knew was that it was what I wanted to eventually accomplish.

I clearly remember that day at the market with my dad, when I stood in front of my first leased office space and admired the name of my business on the plaque. It was a chilly day that day too, and although not cold enough to blow smoke signals in the air, I remembered how it all started, how my little dream became a reality. Yes, it takes hard work and dedication, and I knew nothing really about running a business except what I learned from my dad and at school. He wasn't a big businessman, and I never dreamed of making it big either; I just wanted to run a successful business. I wanted to be my own boss. I wanted to live my dream.

I spent the early years tirelessly working, day in and day out. In the beginning, you wear every hat because there is no other choice. Putting processes in place, contemplating decisions, and weighing endless options. My dad would tell me, I was working too hard; You have your whole life ahead of you, enjoy it, he'd say. His little business made him a little extra money. At nineteen, my business became my bread and butter. I later juggled children, home, extended family, and no doubt, little by little, the burdens accumulated, and stress seeped through from all angles. I had no time for myself. Yet, year after year, when I saw the results, the numbers, and the growth, it all became worth it.

I became responsible and level-headed. I micromanaged, controlled, and persevered. My business taught me a lot of life lessons; it taught me how to deal with people, finances, and myself. I grew with my business, from a teenager to midlife, from debt to self-financing, from no time to being able to balance. I became a leader. The most gratifying feeling is to be able to give a job to someone who needs it. I taught many people what I knew, and perhaps in some insane way, I became a part of their dream. People don't realise that when you support a small business, you're also supporting someone's dream. You're believing in someone's vision, you're contributing to someone's success.

I look back now at the legacy I leave behind, the empire I built, and the people I touched. Three decades later, when I stepped down, I looked back at the building that held my entire dream. I never forgot how I started. I would tell anyone to follow their dream because in anything you set out to do, you can most certainly have a drive and passion and work hard, but if you don't have the dedication and a vision inside you, no one on the outside can manifest it for you. It's better to have a dream fail than kill it without even trying. No one can make smoke signals for you; they come from within at the right time.

Forgiveness

I really never made you work hard for the love I thought you deserved. I made up excuses for myself when you didn't explain yourself. I accepted apologies when they weren't given to me. I tried to see the best in you, even at your worst. I lied for you and even fought for you. While you sat on your throne, your queen admired you with all your faults.

At your worst, I made you a priority so you could feel good about yourself. I put aside my dreams for you. I left my world for you. You didn't even care what was important to me. I didn't make you work hard for my attention. I accepted the love that I thought I deserved, but you took the love you thought you were entitled to.

You never saw me walking behind you, picking up after you. I gave so much of myself without expectations. I gave up so much, even when you couldn't do the same for me. I made time even when you didn't have any left for me. You never saw that it was just your time I needed. You never even noticed the simple life I wanted because you were too busy living your big dream. I was okay with just you. What I wanted you couldn't afford, and yet it was so affordable.

Then one day, I figured it out. I began to argue because I cared. The day I stopped arguing was the day I stopped caring. I stopped arguing, and my silence said it all. You showed me why I no longer belonged in your life. My silence didn't mean anything to you.

This sensitive, insecure individual began surviving without the scraps you were feeding my heart. A heart doesn't just turn to stone overnight. My heart gave up over time. It gave up because at some point, the beating slowed down. Even when you figured it out, it no longer wanted you back. One day, I realized I didn't want it anymore, this life of pretense, ruthlessness, despair and no love. One day, I realized my heart was still beating. And with that frail heart, I left your world.

Now I'm trying to forgive myself for being who I needed to be to accommodate you, for not knowing better. I'm forgiving myself for giving you the power. I'm learning to let go of the hurtful past. I'm forgiving myself for becoming someone weak and intimidated. I'm forgiving myself for enduring the trauma you inflicted on me. I'm trying hard to forgive myself for becoming an imposter. With time, I shall heal and move forward but right now the only thing I cannot forgive is you.

The White Pigeon

I've been awake for some time; the morning light has forced its way into my bedroom. Every dawn it welcomes itself like an unexpected guest. Today, I find it especially hard to face it directly. Yesterday's workout is being felt in my limbs, and getting out of bed will be a workout in itself this morning. So, I lay for a moment longer and morph into my sheets.

My eyes fixate on a pigeon perched on my balcony. It's as white as snow and makes for a great shot, but I savor the moment instead. I recall pigeons being intelligent, and their navigating abilities are commendable. They were used for sending notes. How miraculously whimsical that must have felt. Another time, another era.

I wonder how far it flew all alone. It doesn't seem one bit fazed by its journey. The pleasantness it portrays makes me believe it's quite content perched here, resting from some busyness, I assume. Each day, I, too, keep myself content and busy. I write, and it's not hard; what is hard is sitting still. That is when my thoughts become unstable. At times, the stillness becomes dangerous. In the evenings, when the world is winding down and dusk slowly creeps in. I, too, mellow down into a blissful slumber, but there are nights when sleep doesn't come so easily. Again, it's my thoughts that make way for some uncertainty.

The longer I gaze at this bird, the more comfortable it seems. I suppose you get used to feeling a certain way. It doesn't take long to become accustomed to your environment. We become agreeable to securing shelter and then letting go seems hard. Was it ever cooped up in a cage, I wonder? Did it free itself like me? When you escape, is when you begin living. When nothing is holding you back, when you release from the restraints, that is when your wings spread.

This pigeon is flawless; it's actually pristine. How is that even possible? How does it manage to stay so unspoiled even after all the miles of flying in all kinds of weather and turbulence? The harshness of the environment must have touched its beauty somewhere. There must be some scar or some blemish to show when it tells the story of its journey. Some of our scars are inside, and I reason with that fact, it too may have a tale or two hidden deep down.

I presume my railing is a pit stop for some much-needed alone time. We all need that, sometime, to gather ourselves and observe the environment from afar. Hence, pigeons are lucky; they easily obtain a bird's-eye view. We learn so late to remove ourselves from a situation and look inwards. Yet it's how we recover from the hurdles and become resilient. We could learn so much from our environment, but sometimes we choose to be absorbed in our own pool of worries and the bubble in which we exist.

Perhaps it will fly back to a family, or, like me, is its journey solo? I commend its bravery. I admire its wonderment of flying wherever the winds take it. It's our own judgments, our wrongs and rights, and our consciousness that holds us back. In no time, the little pigeon takes off. I scutter out onto the balcony as if somehow, I could have stopped it. I could just feel its presence, so I breathe in the new air this morning. Silently, I thank the snow-white pigeon for granting me a few minutes of reflection and a little marvel of beauty I witnessed.

The Ring

The subject, "the wedding ring," and I had just finished explaining. I went through three rings during my one marriage. "It should never be removed or replaced," were the words hurled at me, as if I had committed some crime. The words did a darn good job of stirring up fury in me. It was the stupidest comment I had heard, and I felt compelled to explain that my entire body size changed throughout my life, so how on earth did this man think I could keep the same ring on the same finger? For the sake of not making a scene, I got up and walked away.

It infuriated me further; not only was he imposing his insane beliefs upon me, but he knew nothing about me. What bothered me more was that just because the wedding ring changed, my views didn't change with it. The original vow I took with the exchange of my ring still sufficed even when my partner didn't keep up his end of the deal, even when the bond lost its vibrancy, even when the ring was not on my finger. I remained the devoted one.

The second and third time I had to size up and then down, I did it alone. I went out and picked my own ring. I was foolish enough to transfer the original stone to the next ring as if it meant something. By the third ring, the excitement of marriage had worn off, and I was left to remain dutiful solo. At some point, it lost its charm and became just another ring.

The cost was worth more than the actual meaning. The unwavering feelings reminded me that it is actually just a piece of expensive metal that I held dear. The wholeness diminished, and why I continued to replace it, I will never know. I'd forget to put it on, but then there was also a reason why I had removed it in the first place. At times, it suffocated me, and then there were times I'd hold on to it as if it would make the heartbreak less painful. To tell myself a lie and to remind myself I did vow, even though it meant nothing. It resulted in a broken circle that accumulated imperfections.

The "ring" is exchanged within many cultures, together with wedding vows. It's a symbol of your commitment, love, and responsibility to one another and to the ritual of marriage. It symbolizes infinite, eternal love.

In the beginning, you feel almost giddy wearing this piece of metal with a cherry on top, showing it off as if you were the chosen one. It's within this first phase of marriage that you adhere to the true meaning of the ceremony you have just taken part in.

I watch ring exchanges today with a heavy heart. Don't get me wrong, I'm always happy for those who find their happiness in life, but inside I also pray they continue to uphold those vows. We forget that the size of the diamond or the name behind the band has no relevance. What is important is that the giver and the receiver must begin and end on the same page of their story. That the words they speak today should also be respected throughout the book. This ring resembles an infinite source of love and should be honored. It's a durable metal for a reason; it defines a strong bond between two people. The ring finger has a direct connection to the heart, so they say. It's a constant reminder that when you pay tribute to your soulmate, you are always committed.

Yes, there is a meaning to this madness, and yet here I am, ringless and uncommitted now. Society made up this ritual like now there is a divorce ring, one you purchase to make yourself feel better. Does it make you feel better? Does it matter that you bought it? Does it remind you of the ties you no longer have? The ring is just society's way of preaching to you that you're committed.

The wedding ring, or lack of one, should symbolize your own belief in this journey. You are the author of your own story, and the ring is just a gesture. It's a little treasure that reminds us of who we are and that we entered into a marriage of two hearts. Your commitment and your love are held deep in your heart, not in this ring. You have to remain devoted and write your story together because when one skips a page, catching up becomes hard. You shouldn't need a ring to remind you of your dedication and love.

I did gain the courage to go back to ask, "Why? Why should a wedding ring never be removed or replaced?" When a man can remove or replace me with that ring securely on my finger, I have every right too, to change it as I wish.

Little Christmas Tree

"It's just a tree," I tell myself as I unravel the fairy lights that are about to brighten the lifeless, artificial, sad, barely 2 ft pine excuse of a Christmas tree. Every year for the past three years, I've told myself I'd get a proper tree, but every year, I don't have the heart to discard this "Charlie Brown" tree with its lifeless branches. I still remember walking into the store the day I purchased it. The shop did a good job of keeping up with the Christmas spirit as masked shoppers wandered around during our first COVID Christmas. I wanted a tree because it would make my small home feel Christmassy. I wasn't sure if my boys would make it out to visit me, but I wanted to be prepared. The underlying truth was, I didn't know if I could afford a proper tree or even if I wanted it, and I didn't know how I would make it through this Christmas, alone.

As I walked through the aisles, I found myself feeling mixed emotions. My first Christmas alone. I am wandering around like a stray dog watching others bask in the season of joy. I watch the shoppers as they fill their carts, and I have nothing desirable drawing me in. Everything here seems to leave me sad and sickly. The mask around my face will do another job today. It will hide my pain and subdued spirit. The Christmas spirit seems to have left my senses, yet watching the colors of the season wrapped on everything I pass lifts me a tad, and then just as quickly, I go back to feeling indisposed.

There's a slight vibe in the air, of appreciation that we all made it to Christmas this year with the pandemic almost behind us. For some of us, it was more than a pandemic; it was a shocking displacement of virtue and the surfacing of many truths that we lied to ourselves about. The principles of a life that still needed to be lived came to us through the heartbreak of seeing that there was more to this disaster than what swept the world. Our priorities needed re-evaluating; to just slow down and focus meant the rising of bitter truths. We were all panicky, some terrified, as we watched and listened to the passing of ones who couldn't fight. Some like me accepted it, and I became undisturbed. It was the harshness that taught me to live in calmness; what will be will be. If I'm meant to pull through, I will. Just like my past life, I'd make it through. But now, even the pandemic seems minuscule compared to what life has thrown my way.

My fingers glide across the bright tissue paper. How things have changed. I would buy rolls of Christmas paper because every gift needed to look unique. I didn't care so much about receiving gifts, but I made sure everyone received one. I'd spend hours wrapping to perfection, decorating my humble abode, and entertaining my loved ones. It seems like another lifetime now. It was all about the children, but they grew up and left. I'd still make the effort, just for them.

Every Christmas, I find a cause worthy of my giving. I helped the less privileged; it was about bringing hope and joy to those who needed my smile. How can you shift through this season and not bring a little bliss to another soul? Christmas satisfied a hunger in me to please, no matter what I was dealing with. This Christmas, I am finding it hard to even please myself.

The aroma of pine filled the air, and my fireplace was decorated specifically for the season, and nestled together under my eight-foot, glistening tree were the presents I had neatly wrapped. I made such an effort to bring everyone together, inviting them into my world of Christmas spirit. I admire the stunningly decorated trees on display. They remind me of the war we had trying to put up my tree and then take it down. It was part of my tradition. Like the ornaments I collected, each one held a story. I smile, remembering my fight with the millions of lights I untangled, together with the ritual of burning one batch of baked goodies.

Christmas cards line the shelves, and I envision myself again comfortably seated for my yearly tradition of handwriting greetings to people I value. I'd sit with my favorite Christmas cup and some morsels of delicate chocolate, singing along to the carols. My mind wanders to the cold evenings we'd be all bundled up. As a little girl, I would sing my heart out as we went door to door with friends and sang carols we learned at school that season. Christmas was treasured even if all you had was just your sweet voice to share.

I pass by the glistening tinsel and the aroma of scented candles, but I have no delight in bringing any of it home. How does your demeanor change towards something that once brought you so much joy? The Christmas staples reminded me of my dining table neatly dressed for the season. My best china made it to the table, the crystals shone in the candlelight, and I was always so proud of my display. I was now reluctant to celebrate and unwilling to let my mood shift. Somehow inside of you, you find the strength to keep going, to move forward, because in the end, we do matter, and life is an adjustment; we either change, or we become stuck.

I take a second glance at a small tree, which is hidden behind some chaos on the shelf; it looks out of place and reminds me of myself. It's not a Christmas tree, but it will do. I evaluate it as if I'm purchasing a luxury brand, then without another thought, it comes home with me. This little tree taught me how much to appreciate what I have. I've rescued something that others found unimportant and lifeless. Something that was alone and needed some care. My little Christmas tree and I made it through my first Christmas. As I continue to dress it up for the season this evening, I know I will never let it go. It's my reminder that when I had lost hope, I found a way, and isn't this what Christmas is all about? Hope and joy.

How to Unlove

No one shows your heart how to love, but then isn't that what hearts just do? My heart was a pure organ; delicate, naïve, and inexperienced. Love just happens, they told me. Slowly, you took, and hesitantly, I gave. The motion of taking and giving grew until one day I did it without a thought. Effortlessly. Like your breath, each inhale and exhale they shift with ease, one after the other. I began to love like I breathed, steadily, fluently.

Then, one day, the gray clouds gathered above, and I chose to ignore the gloominess. The overcast spoke silently. I disregarded the signs. Not because I wasn't aware, but because I was comfortable sharing and giving. I was breathing just fine, effortlessly.

Without a signal, the storm rocked my existence, and I was left staring out at nothingness. Numb to my own thoughts and to the wounds that appeared. I was unsure what broke first, my heart or my soul. One after the other, the pieces tore apart. The morsels continued to fall as I tried to gather them, but I was buried deep. With each piece, I bled deeper.

I grieved, anger set in, and I fought with denial, and just like the process demanded, depression overpowered. I bargained with guilt. Just as you mourn death, I mourned the parts of my heart that had no pulse, the parts that were silenced, the parts I couldn't bring back to life.

I no longer wanted the give and take; it revolted me. I gave love in abundance because it satisfied me, and yet I rarely asked. I withdrew from taking it because I felt selfish. The scraps you fed my heart were enough for me to survive on until you mocked my innocence. Your harsh, derisive blows demeaned my empathic soul.

I was tired from the never-ending blows. I was exhausted from continuously trying to pick up my broken pieces. The final stage is acceptance, so they say, except I didn't master this stage. My heart changed with this episode. You see, with each soul who sets foot within these boundaries now, it becomes an intruder. Acceptance means I'm willing. I bargained with the paradox of tolerance. Tolerance demands discomfort, and I'm not ready to be uncomfortable again.

I wanted to go back in time, to the place where my virgin heart was left to beat alone, silently, rhythmically. Now, emotional intimacy seems much harder than it is because it involves exposing pieces of my damaged organ. Tying strings means compromises, expectations, and loyalty, and my heart isn't ready to display such traits.

I ponder from time to time. How many hearts have torn like mine, how many mended, how many just settled, and how many hearts continue to bleed a slow, agonizing death? I moved on from the endless giving. The scars will remain, but the aftermath left a different version of me. A toughened heart, one that still manages to beat and yet somehow foolishly yearns to be loved. My heart was never taught how to love. Love, they told me, just happens. And as easily as that, I have taught myself how to unlove.

In Control

I sink into the water, my limbs surrender, and the perfect temperature encapsulates every inch of my skin. The tiny grains beneath my feet allow me to grip on while the playful but forceful waves try hard to tug at me. I'm in awe of these vast waters, the same ocean, a different place. My eyes scan effortlessly, intrigued by the clarity that's allowing me to see deep down to the seabed. Just like my life, I see it clearly. Sea life passes by me as if I'm non-existent, and I find I have an immense liking for this solidarity.

The longer I float, I begin to analyze. There's nothing but water, and yet strangely, it's helping me unravel the complexities of life. I find I have little control here; if the waves became powerful, the water would control me.

We all live with some kind of mania, some form of psychotic behavior. Not many of us want to admit to our flaws. It's the murky waters that we find hard to step into, and yet we expect someone to follow us into our pool, which is anything but translucent.

It's having control that gives us power. Having the ability to be able to shift a mind, even if it's just a little. This small victory subconsciously results in an opportunity for reign. Those who depend on you can control you. They do it innocently. The subtle ways in which you give in because they matter more than you; they own that power. At times, I wanted to be controlled as much as I wanted to control. It was a false sense of trust and a small dose of manipulation. I mistook it for caring until I figured out that control can also be a deadly weapon.

If I were to lose my grip and let the water take me away, it would dominate my life. I am nothing compared to the force around me, and in this same way, I was once swayed by people. The jurisdiction over my mind caused havoc. It was these same waters I would have chosen to drown in, to get away from the emotional trauma.

It's this very control that scares me now. The reason I grip harder and put up my guards, and the reason I failed, is that I did not pay attention to the noise around me. My past taught me how not to fall into a trap of influence. I observe and I walk away before an interaction even begins. I feel the energy now, and I transcend from it. Self-realization happens when your mood doesn't shift, and you follow your instinct.

As my own body shifts in the water and I, myself, lose some control, I steady myself, entering into a realm of some kind of stoicism; I realize I also don't want to control the world. I cannot control the world, only how I respond. Just as we can't control nature, we only control how we respond to it. Being immersed here awakens me to the idea of drifting away and the fact that these waters could also leave me still and lifeless. I've felt that way before, sinking into nothingness, and so I leave behind what isn't serving me.

Control happens when you begin to give in to your desires and hand over your reins. You grant permission and slowly begin to tolerate the suffering. I've mistaken control with feeling safe. One makes you feel so managed that letting go enacts a kind of disintegration. When in fact, being protected is an entirely different chapter. For fear of losing, we'd rather be controlled. We become accustomed to the comfort of a kind, and venturing out of that zone is anything but comfortable.

As I turn to gaze at the horizon, no obstruction lies in our path. All I see is the sky and the sea and the fine line where we are seduced into believing they meet. It's an illusion, a make-believe scene. Just like the many tales we are made to believe. Then there are stories we make up in our heads to satisfy that side of us that is restrained or the side that wants to believe in a dream.

As I lose the grip from beneath my feet, I use my ability to swim in the direction of a less controlled force. Not one person on this earth is so high that they have a right to look down on me. Not one person walks this earth without a flaw. So that supremacy belongs to no one. Control happens when we allow it. Not one person on this earth has the right to direct your mind, and so I rethink the situations, and the conversations, and perhaps I overthink.

I make it to shore, and as I leave the deep sea, I feel my weight shift. It takes me a minute to become accustomed to gravity, and don't we all, for some time, feel uneasy. As I turn around and face the horizon, the discomfort wears off. It's that fine line that taught me freedom prevails. I walk away, feeling liberated, unapologetic, and uncontrolled.

Distance Makes the Heart Grow Fonder

This phrase, I learned the meaning of it so young. When distance pulls you away from the only love you know, your heart does grow fonder. Just like the words I write, the memories remain even when I try to erase them; they appear just like the lost love. Like an old book that was forgotten but well read, I will always remember our story. I have unwritten chapters of my book and blank pages; my pen awaits.

I don't know what I gain from wanting something that is not so easily obtainable. I try hard to console my heart, but it walks astray as if it, too, is upset with me for the miles between us. It wasn't intended, it just happened, and now all I have are the words, the blank pages, and memories to hold on to, and the sweet sound of your voice on occasion, and once in a while, I am worthy of your presence. When my soul spends time at your side, I feel whole. But that same sum of time that distance stole from me is what I yearn for now. Even with the distance between us, I couldn't steal time.

I wait in anticipation for the day I can see the sparkle in your eyes and hear your voice in person. I wait for the stories and the embrace, and most of all, I wait to see how life has treated you without me. I want to hear how your time passed away from the one who loves you entirely. Quietly and patiently, I wait for you to tell me you, too, missed me just a little, perhaps, but that I was missed.

My heart does grow fonder, being here alone. It seemed to realize how precious you are. My love for you grows without even trying, and I don't know how, but I cease to see the imperfections in you now. Distance taught me to savor the sweetness, to let go of the little mishaps and the disagreements. The flaws don't matter to me anymore. Distance taught me that every moment is precious. Living a life without the love I deserved allowed me to grow fond of you, little by little, a new you transpired for me. Just like that, you became much more important.

Tomorrow, I plan, and yesterday, I longed, but what do I do today when the agony of not having you here becomes unbearable? Distance has made me tough; it's made the goodbyes a little less painful. It taught me, we ultimately walk alone. My eyes scan your pictures as I pass by, and some days tears drop, and you are worth every tear I cry. Other days, I smile, and it is that same happiness that makes me proud to have you in my life.

Yes, my child, I gave birth to you, but you were never mine to keep for eternity. Having a child is a privilege, but you are not my property. I gave birth to a life, and eventually that life lives for its own. We forget, children pass through us, but they own their destiny. Distance taught me that the sooner I accept this truth, the sooner I can appreciate what I raised. I won't lie, I have been selfish, wanting you for myself, but I cannot fulfill every desire I wish.

Embracing change and enjoying the meaningful peace I have obtained without wanting more, that is enough happiness. I gave you wings, and you flew. Now my wishes are for you to soar to new heights. All I can ask of you is to never forget, the one who birthed you is always waiting, and even with the distance between us, I hope your heart, too, grows fonder.

Worth a Celebration

I'm escorted through the dining area to my table in a corner. I thank the waiter and get comfortable in the booth; it's perfect. Away from the crowd. Why I prefer to be secluded, I still don't know. There are a lot of things about me I still haven't figured out. I check my phone, and my company is running late. As I accept a glass of water, I gaze around. The music pairs nicely with my surroundings, and the ambience stimulates my need to celebrate something. My eyes fixate on a couple. They seem happier than most middle-aged couples I've seen. It delights me to know they're glowing, probably empty nesters, out on a date. I wonder if they have a secret to their obsession. A magic potion I didn't know about, that allows them to tolerate each other's company still. As I chuckle to myself, I begin to realize my insanity. I should know better; I don't know their story, but it does little to draw me away, and I speculate anyway.

Her face seems jovial, and he seems to care. He reaches for her hand, and I see the attentiveness in his touch. He probably assisted in choosing her dress, telling her how the aqua color complemented her hair. Most likely gifted her the beautiful diamond studs that sparkle in the candlelight. Just before they left the house, he probably pulled her towards him and told her how beautiful she looked. That's it, all we want really. Someone to pay attention to us and tell us how much we are valued and how our efforts to look pretty are not overlooked. The wear and tear on our figures shouldn't take away from the care that still lives in our hearts.

He probably carried her coat, opened the door, and made her feel like a queen. You don't have to own a crown just to know that you deserve one. The smile lines indented in his bearded face tell me her spoken words humored him. It's the little conversations, the meaningless subjects that humor us the most, and that is what tends to die first. We want to laugh again, let loose, and be amused, but what happens? When do the simple things become irritating? When does life become so serious and a train of never-ending wants and needs that can't be fulfilled?

I observe them as they discuss the menu options together, and I see the excitement in her eyes as she scans the menu. No one is ordering for her, or even just ordering her for that matter. It's all we want, isn't it? Someone to sit beside you and allow you to be yourself. Someone to hug you tightly and tell you they'll always be there right beside you. Someone to wish you a good morning and good night. Someone to gaze at your heavenly face and make you feel like there is no other more important.

What we craved all along is what we figure out later in life. It's not the materialistic things, it's such simple, mindful, painless efforts. Comfort food, a touch, a few words, a companion. We outgrow the need to be controlled by our surroundings. It's not a race anymore. We look around for the need to sit on the side and just take a breath. With time, it becomes so pertinent.

He pours for her, pulls her chair, kisses her cheek. We want that respect, the same care, attention, and someone's time. I wanted to feel important, worthy even. The neglect, disregard, and unfavored responses fueled my existence, and now I just watch something I never had. The candle on my table flickers as another couple passes by. It reminds me of how hard we try to keep the flame from burning out; it becomes so much harder than we want to believe. Every relationship has its ups and downs. Then comes a time when we have to decide if lighting the candle again is going to be worth the effort.

As I glance up from my menu, I see their wine glasses being filled. We pour our everything into relationships in the beginning, and then life happens. We begin to take one another for granted, and in that illusion, we miss the importance of the value of another human being. They toast, perhaps to good health and happiness, and I silently wish the same for them. Everyone deserves happiness and to be celebrated, whether you belong beside another or you travel solo. Your worth does not diminish because you were not valued. It decreases when you don't value yourself, and we are all worth a celebration!

I Believe

I am a believer that all things happen for a reason. The universe has energy that is reflected around your aura. I believe in the stars and that when the planets align, they pass energy to us. If the moon can move the oceans, then why not for us?

I believe in vibes, and I listen to my inner consciousness. I feel the energy, and I am aware of my surroundings. I believe everything falls into place as it should. Time makes you wise; you're not older but wiser. Your body heals, but your mind remembers. Too much noise can alter your character, and no noise helps you filter into the core of your spirit.

Emotions need to be released to move on, and letting go isn't always a bad thing. For you to grow, you have to release the attachment. Negativity will always dampen the season; regretting shouldn't be allowed. I believe everything happens for a reason, because the universe decides when you are ready and when you're not.

We learn from all the bad things because we need to learn those lessons. Your past is what you grew from, and someone can always learn from you. Internalizing issues only slows you down. Step back from disturbances and let them unfold, for you cannot control them or another person's emotions. Your shoes are not made for someone else to walk in. Know your path and don't expect someone to understand why you chose it.

Expect nothing; you will be better for it, free from disappointment. Live in the present. Even if it's just sitting around alone, own your space. Move your body, explore yourself, take care of your limbs, your complexion, and your spirit. Radiate your smile and flavor the spaces you visit. Own yourself, have confidence in your abilities, and don't let anyone change the ambience you thrive in. Manifest positive vibes. Transformation is a wonderful awakening. Your behavior speaks volumes.

It has not only a purpose but also values too. Your wisdom is your biggest asset. Cultivate kindness, be an inspiration, a mentor, and it will take you to a higher level of gratification. Make way for good things, cultivate your seeds, and let yourself grow. I believe in fate, and that our road is already paved. There are two things out of your control: time and death. We all need to learn to breathe deeply, inhale the goodness, and exhale the negative. Master how to stay calm. Let the sun shine on your face and sit under a full moon. Let them both radiate on you. Let their energy reflect on your aura. Believe that everything will be ok.

Don't Look Back

Don't look back, I won't be waiting for you. You may see my faded silhouette, but beneath the fog, there lies no soul. She moved on. You only see an illusion of what you perceive. We all seem to find it hard to let go of things we become accustomed to. Material things can be replaced. You can't replace a soul; we're irreplaceable. Find a way to let me go.

If I had taken you for granted, then it would be hard for me, too. You see, I became able and willing. All those years ago, when you chose to disregard, you unknowingly nudged me down this very path. The little steps became bigger strides, and before you knew it, I was part of another world.

I didn't permit my ego to overpower my aura. I chose empathy over ego. I choose compassion over spite. I never allowed that behavior to enter my atmosphere. I couldn't watch one suffer, yet I never saw you as a threat to my misery. You forget how you treated another human in your anguish. Unmeant words still tarnish, long after they are spoken; they still hover over the wounds. You forget the words that broke a spirit. You simply forget.

Do you know what self-sabotage looks like? You should have gazed at me a while longer. If you had focused a little harder on the parts of me that didn't resonate with you, you would have had a glimpse of how prematurely that side of me wilted. A glimpse of my heart would have shown you how quickly it morphed into stone. I admit that at times, the hurt became so piercing that I wasn't sure I would make it. The wounds became so raw, but tolerance, too, is a mighty trait. It wasn't hard for me, moving on. When the wretched mistreatments were set aside, one walks a path of solitude with ease. Because like everything else in life, it came to go.

Karma says you will be hurt over and over again by the same person until you learn the lesson of letting go. Don't look back, I won't be there waiting. I let karma hold my hand, and it led the way, and that is how easily I let go. I don't look back because it's not where I'm going.

An Arranged Marriage

I remember sitting on the bed, watching my mother break down. She never cried, even when my father and she fought. She made herself tough through anything, like a tiger. She was my bold and beautiful heroine, so seeing her cry made me feel overwhelmed with helplessness. I was confused. She wanted this, so why was she so upset? I didn't dare to ask for fear of the unknown. I was scared of the unknown. The lump in my throat blocked my voice, and so I cried because she cried. I sat and cried with her. We held each other for what seemed like hours.

I wanted to ask her, why was she ok with sending me away to another land? Why was she ok with marrying me off this young, and why was she ok with giving me away to a stranger and his family? Her sobbing told me she wasn't entirely satisfied with her decision. Then why was she releasing me into the wild when all my life she sheltered and protected me like a tiger protects her cub? Except I didn't grow up to be a tiger. I was nothing like her. I was a young, naïve, vulnerable, innocent teen.

I was being ushered out of the nucleus to start a life with someone I barely knew. I would leave the two people who lovingly brought me into this world. My role as a daughter, sister, niece, cousin, and friend would somewhat cease. I was given a new part in another play without a script. I had a performance but no training, no practice, no guarantee, no rights even and there was no return.

I wanted to gather every tear that fell from her tender face and give them back to her. It was too late now, the decision was made, and she was now carelessly regretting her steps in that very decision she supported. She was going to feel the absence of her firstborn because that absence would leave a void only a mother can feel. It happened to her, and so it would happen to me. I don't blame my parents. They didn't know better;, they were doing justice by their culture and tradition. My parents knew very well, I'd be the gold that brought wealth to the family that was waiting. They knew without the slightest hesitation that I'd do as I was told. I always made my parents proud because I did as I was told. But they overlooked the part where my absence would haunt them. It would tear them apart when they would give their little girl away to a stranger.

My feelings didn't seem to matter much; it was in my best interest and in the best interest of the families involved. My emotions were set aside like the suitcase that lay neatly packed for my departure. My new life will bring me happiness, and I can do whatever I want after I get married, they told me. How could they be so certain? How can one human not only decide but also predict another human's fate?

I didn't understand the complexity of it all, the arranged marriage. I was told, ultimately it was my choice, but is it a choice when you know that if you don't abide, you would become a reject? If I had said no, I would have been hurled back to the drawing board once again because I was born a girl. I came with an expiration date. It's that submissiveness that girls of my generation and culture can relate to. In the end, it is your choice, they told me. But then why did it feel like a demand that didn't permit a refusal? Declining the offer would make me feel like I insulted their integrity. I trusted them with my life. So, I decided for everyone involved except me. I made a sacrifice, one of many I made on this journey I was about to embark on.

It is an arranged marriage that predicts the fate of a girl. It's an arrangement between two families that think they know what's best for a young child. It's the parents who decide for her, right from wrong. It's a society, culture, religion, even, that dictates an alignment of values for an innocent being. None of these people will walk in my shoes. None of them will compromise, live, or suffer with me.

My wedding was a small affair in a foreign land where I knew no one. I had no say in anything. I was dressed to play a role. I sat silently and did what I was told. I knew my future husband for barely a few months; he seemed nice, but my shy, introverted, innocent self had no experience in courting. They would expect me to morph from a girl to a woman overnight, from a teen to a wife. They expected me to be content with my new life as they handed me over to someone they themselves didn't know.

Now and again, my eyes would search through the many strangers that stood amongst me for that one familiar face. On my wedding day, I constantly searched for the face that I would no longer see every day. Who would I turn to in my time of need? Who would I trust? My mother would glance back. Her glistening eyes and the fake smile would turn away instantly because only we knew that the next tear that would fall would be the one that reminded her that she chose to give me away.

I won't lie, there was some excitement in starting over in a different country, but it left a distaste, feelings similar to those of an abandoned cub. I would carve my future, but at the cost of another authority controlling it. I would discover the secrets of a predetermined union and unravel the myths of a so-called happily arranged marriage. The price I paid for that moment's decision was dear to say the least. It was a gamble of sorts, but when reality began to sink in, it became a rollercoaster of saga, misbeliefs, and at times punishment.

It took me years to come to terms with destiny. You try your hardest to live blissfully. We all become comfortable in our lives, but some of us have no idea in which direction we're headed, because someone decided to write out our fate for us. We gladly accepted the challenge because fighting it would mean we would be chastised for committing a crime.

My Father's Diary

I was accompanied to the hospital to pick up my late father's belongings. "What belongings?" I thought to myself. They don't belong to anyone anymore. Occasionally, I would look over at my younger siblings, wondering where they were getting their strength from and why I was finding it hard to stay put together. Death brings out another form of you; one you don't recognize. These thoughts occupied my mind on this endless journey back to the hospital.

It was daunting to go back to the same building where my father lost his fight to live. Along with his death certificate and a bag, the hospital staff handed me a diary. My dad's name was handwritten on the front. It seemed a little peculiar how now he was just a name. From the day he set foot into the emergency room until he passed in the Intensive Care Unit, every day for over a month, the nurse in charge wrote in this diary. A documentation of my dad's progress, or lack of, as he slowly maneuvered from life to death.

At first, I thought it was a thoughtful gesture. It wasn't until I opened the pages and began to comprehend what was inscribed that I realized this was an etched piece of painful history. With each word I read, I began to re-draw the scene I had tried so hard to forget. Memories of the Critical Care Ward flooded back, and the image of his helpless body fighting for life filled my vision. The sounds of the monitors echoed in my ears, and for a moment, it seemed like I was right there at his bedside. I could smell that sterile hospital odor, the pale walls that matched the gray floors. The white coats that shift from one patient to the next. The ticking of the clock that hung in solitary confinement. I was right there again, watching him in a deep slumber with a blurred vision, a prayer in thought, and the sickly massacre brewing in my stomach of not knowing the outcome. I heard again the unforgiving beeps of the machines that were keeping him from taking his last breath. I remembered the painful decision of having to let him go.

“Your family has been sitting at your side, they are praying for you,” the diary read. I sometimes wondered if he even knew I was there. Or any one of the familiar faces that also waited their turn to see him. Faces of despair would pay visits, and at times, I wanted to tell them all to go home. There was no room for more misery. Even as he lay there with no recollection, I prayed because he was with me in body. I could tell him things even if he couldn't hear me. At least I could hold his hand and feel the warmth of his fatherly figure.

Each day as the lights went out, we too would bid him farewell. The following morning, we’d greet him, holding hope’s hand, only to discover it too was giving up. I didn’t want to lose hope; hope left him. It left because he had no will left in him to try. His time had come, and even though I knew, it was still hard to say that final goodbye. The one where you are left wondering what you did to deserve this, you are left wondering why you were chosen to lose yet another parent.

His death taught me that the kind words that are being said now should have been echoed when life existed. We never speak ill of one who is preparing for transition to the next world. Yet during one’s life, we aren't so forgiving, are we? Life takes on a whole other meaning when you are at death’s bedside. Yet somehow it still seems like a selfish encounter; you don’t want them to go because you will be the one left alone. Left to pick up the pieces of a story that didn’t end in your favor.

Each sentence in the diary hit me like a bullet initially, but it showed how hard everyone tried, even the ones that didn't know him. They meant nothing, but they did their job of making him comfortable. The nurses who knew not one thing about his life were brave enough to write about his last days. "I see your family so sad as you are passing, rest in peace." When he entered a coma, I knew we wouldn't get him back. I had that gut feeling that never leaves, even when you try to fight it. When I sat beside him, I wondered how his absence would make me feel. I didn't want him to suffer, but did I want this?

Death is an ultimate test, cruel and painful, yes, but for those left to deal with the absence, death becomes a test of your own life. The key to dealing with death is acceptance. The sooner we are willing to acknowledge that the process is a part of our existence, that it's the final path we all must walk, the sooner we can pass through our own life with some gratitude. Being thankful that we, too, have a life that was in some insane way meant to be a part of the departed. Accept that it is a privilege to know those we loved, and accept what is when they transition to the next phase.

It was gut-wrenching to read what they had documented in my father's diary, and now there's nothing left but these pages and memories and my gratitude that I was a part of his life. My father used to tell me that we enter this world alone, and alone is how we will go. "Practice detachment," he'd say. As I sat there in silence, holding his hand and waiting for him to breathe his last breath, that is when I understood his message.

Reflect

My eyes open, meeting floor-to-ceiling windows that let in the gloominess of the gray sky. For a minute, I wonder where I am, then I realize I'm far from home, snuggled in a Sherpa blanket, protecting myself from the dull chill in the air. It's not daybreak yet, and the bleak sky dulls my mood further. I came to a place from my past. The atmosphere did a grand job of painting the picture for me. Need I say more, but it is how I left it, gray, a little morbid, uninviting.

The anxiety that was building up over the last few days beckoned me into a form of alignment. Like the picture frame that sits on the floor here, waiting to be hung. It tells me it's not your time yet; you still need to heal. You're not quite ready to be displayed. And so I reflect, will these visits get easier for me? Will I, at some point, come back and feel nothing? I managed to disconnect, or should I say, distance myself so as to recover mentally. But do you ever become a younger version, one that wasn't so tarnished? The same streets I knew like the back of my hand seem almost foreign now. They lead to no place I want to be.

The chill surrounds me like an unfamiliar ocean. Some nights I do feel as if I will drown. It's that sense of not belonging. This same feeling arose when I walked into my parents' house without them; it's not where I belong anymore. For fear of losing any connection with the ones I loved, I wander back here, yet I feel like a wanderer who has no home.

I have built a home elsewhere now, that is my home, and this used to be. I'm alone, and loneliness offers nothing to the one who has mastered solitude. I find myself in deeper thought here, thoughts that I spent so long eliminating. They came back one by one. Now my mind is confused. The new me was happier where I rebuilt my life. Oh, how I worked on myself to bring out the best in me. I still search for pieces of my past, so here, the old me travels back. I don't want to resonate with that version of me anymore, but the more I fight it, the more it leads.

It is here, as I lie and watch the gloominess transform into dawn, that I understand that you cannot let go of your past. It's a part of who you are. It's how you became the current version of yourself. Your past is history, good or bad; it is just a memory. We need to learn to dissect them, put the painful ones to rest, and be thankful you have happy memories to hold on to. This process is what has to be practiced.

My present and future should not be impacted by my past but rather remembered as lessons that made me resilient. I was given a chance to make this change in my life, and this new phase was used to rebuild my future. It's only I who can choose what part of my past I want to revisit. I get to choose the happy memories that travel with me.

I stare at the picture frame a moment longer, and it looks different now. The daylight shines on it, and I conclude that, like me, it's a work in progress; someday it will hang like a piece that belongs in a gallery. One that will tell a story of bygones, and when the eyes that set on it see the version that transpired into something beautiful, may they not overlook the work that went into creating this masterpiece.

PART V

The Ordinary that Shapes

Seasons shift, we find contentment in small moments, comfort in familiar things. No mystery to unfold - simplicity is the true essence of life.

- It Takes a Village Page 158
- The Little Beggar Girl Page 161
- I'm Sorry Page 163
- In My Car Page 166
- Separation Page 169
- Cry If You Want To Page 172
- My Neighbor Val Page 175
- Soul Sister Page 179
- Welcome to My Home Page 181
- The Strays Page 183
- Agree to Disagree Page 185
- The Gentlemen's Club Page188
- My Cutting-Edge Phone Page 191
- Take a Ride with Me Page 194
- You Crossed My Path Page 197

It Takes a Village

"Mom, Mom, Mom!" The same word repeated at times would make me cringe. On the other hand, it's also the one word you never want to stop hearing. Mothering gives you a sense of purpose. It's a meaningful role, and I was a Supermom. I did it all. Nothing was unattainable, unfixable, or impossible. I handled it all, and mostly I did it alone. I was that one "go to" person that my children needed. I became the person I didn't have growing up.

Eventually, your children grow up and find themselves friends and new relations, and then they move out into the big, wide world. My children found other "go to" people, and without even knowing it, I became an afterthought. I held the third, fourth, and fifth place in line. I never thought it was possible to be not so dependable anymore.

They say it takes a village to raise a child, but as a young mother, I didn't quite believe it. Not until they grew up. Not until something so profound happens do we realize that it does take a village. You can't always be there, you can't always hear their cries for help, and you can't always fix everything.

When distance set in, I tried harder than I had ever done before to stay in touch. Even when I was hurt by them, I reached out. I set aside my ego and my respected role and addressed a communication gap that so many parents miss. I thought I was doing everything right. The truth is, parents fill a wider gap in a child's early years, and when they grow up, others fill the gap that we parents refuse to see or acknowledge. Unknowingly, they reach out to others for guidance, because we can't be there, or we sometimes become ignorant.

So when an issue arises, instead of acting on impulse, ask yourself what choices they have. If they chose a path unaligned with yours, it's because they are not you. We are quick to be judgmental, but that's not what they need, and perhaps it's a reason you weren't the first shoulder in line. Perhaps they, too, are protecting you, or maybe you should ask yourself why you weren't there.

I commend the friends and teachers who fill those blank spaces. The voids that need attention. I raise my hat to the role models in every child's life that help make them feel heard and supported. The people our children turn to because we can't be there. Our own lives are demanding and stressful, and we don't see the silent cues, or we disregard an important aspect. This is their life. Every human is unique, and children are no different.

When I'm not there battling for them, I hope there is someone my child looks up to. Someone they can turn to in their time of need, and someone who can understand why they can't reach out to me. We teach our children to grow wings and fly, and we teach them to be independent and strong. It's a cruel world, and we give them the means to survive out there. We teach them the very things that ultimately wound us.

I'm proud of my children. I'm proud of the mother I am. I'm also proud of the ones who were there for them because I couldn't be. It does take an entire community to contribute to many aspects of a child's well-being, be it socially, emotionally, or intellectually. It does take an entire village to raise a child, and it takes special people to accept them for who they are.

The Little Beggar Girl

Even when I'm not traveling to this part of the world, I wonder why everyone is not on the same level. Why couldn't we all be the same in terms of standards, values, and living? Why are some so sickly rich and others devastatingly poor? We share a planet, and it doesn't mean a thing; we were all dealt different cards, and that makes me sad.

As I leaned my head against the car window, I watched the crowds of people, some of them are so simple here, they go about their business, only interested in the income they'll take home that day. Some of them sit in luxury vehicles, unaware of their surroundings, because they have too much.

We stopped at a traffic signal, and I was approached by a little human. I was always told to ignore the beggars; if you feed one, they all come. But in this moment, my heart melted at the sight before me, and with consent, I pulled down the car window. She was selling balloons. Her brown honey touched tangled hair matched her big brown eyes, and her skin was bronzed by the Delhi sun. It seemed as if water hadn't touched it for days. She had perfect little features that were tarnished with dust. Her petite stature was carried by dirty little feet; they caught your eye because the only accessory was the anklets that wrapped her frail ankles. She wore a gray, tattered dress.

Unlike the rest of the street sellers, she didn't say a word. But her eyes said everything. She shoved the balloons towards the window, and I lost her for a minute. She instantly pushes them aside, and I try to guess her age, maybe five. I shook my head to turn down the offer for the balloon as I handed over a bill. I watched her magnetic chocolate eyes light up as she grabbed the note from my hand. She pulled it towards her chest and held onto it tightly.

For a split moment, I felt as if I had aided in making her life, yet this simple act had probably just made her day. Her frail body turned and skipped barefoot, dodging through the traffic, and I felt both happiness and sadness. This exchange of emotions and money cost me nothing.

My thoughts transported me to a place where I saw her in school instead of on the street, and I imagined her groomed and transformed into a version of pretty that she deserved. I want to do more. I want to help in non-monetary ways, be hands-on, teach these girls the importance of an education, and get them off the streets. For now, all I could do was thank myself for this humbling experience that, once in a while, needs to be instilled so I can be thankful for everything I have. Every day is a chance for me to pay gratitude to the universe that the life I live is a deserving one and that helping the less fortunate shouldn't be a choice but a duty.

I'm Sorry

While trying to exit a building and balancing on my crutches with a booted foot, a stranger carelessly bumped into me. He caught me off guard, and my friend held on to me to avoid another mishap. The stranger and I both apologized simultaneously. My friend was annoyed at the interaction and asked me why I said sorry. "I don't know," I exclaimed. Why was I sorry?

It got me thinking. What exactly was I sorry about? That he bumped into me? Or that I was partially disabled at the time? Or was it that I was sorry because I made his life uneasy at that moment? All of the above reasons don't require an apology on my part.

I say sorry out of habit, because I feel it's my fault when in fact I'm not at fault. I wasn't being pitiful or remorseful, or saying it even out of despair. It's funny how unconsciously we say and do things out of habit. We subject ourselves to mindless acts of some proportion every day. Others notice, and we have blindly become accustomed to them.

I know when to say please and thank you, just like everyone else, just like I had been taught by my parents. When we say these words, I was taught we should mean them, from deep inside. I was taught to say sorry to be apologetic for something I did wrong. "Sorry" is for consoling and understanding and regretting that you made a mistake, accepting that you were wrong. It's supposed to be a meaningful gesture.

So, what happened? I began to say sorry out of habit. I presume it's because throughout my life, I've never received an apology for all the wrongs people did to me. When you have to move on from relationships in life, absent an apology, you succumb to a guilt-ridden affair of your own. Their egotistical behavior got in the way, and I wasn't worth an apology, and so I moved on, ashamed that the disheartening, vulnerable state I was left in would allow for some closure of my own.

With time, I learned that waiting around for someone to be apologetic was a waste of my time. You cannot expect solicitude from everyone. Not everyone is forgiving. I also figured out that accepting an apology meant I was okay with the wrongs, and deep down, I wasn't ok with the destruction. When too much time passes, so does the level of trust diminish. An apology is accepting, understanding, and validating feelings. It means you took responsibility for your actions. You understand you hurt someone, and you regret it; most of all, you mean it. So instead, I made up for all the apologies I never received. It's become so embedded in me that now I don't think twice when it rolls over my tongue. I'm just sorry.

I say sorry when someone drops something, when someone has to walk past me, and even when they bump into me. I'm sorry that I was in the way or they made a mistake because, in some small, insane way, I was a part of that interaction that required an apology. I'm sorry because even if they don't apologize, I did it for them. Could it also be that I am a compassionate person? I look above and beyond, and instead of waiting for the apology, I set my ego aside and became a bigger person, and I apologize instead. Because if I don't get that apology, I have one for you to give to me. I have your apology right here, waiting.

My friend rolled her eyes at me. "You need to stop saying sorry for everything," she blurted. 'It wasn't even your fault!' I'm mindful now. It'll take a while for me to cease being sorry for something you did to me, or maybe I'll never let go of my "sorries," because my little ego doesn't get in the way of an apology. I'm sorry.

In My Car

I throw my handbag onto the passenger seat as I sink into mine. I slowly release the keys into the cup holder. I take a few deep breaths as I rest my hands on the steering wheel. I pull down the visor, even though the view is pleasant enough ahead; my eyes want to close. My limbs release into the leather seat that has molded to my figure. What is it about sitting in your car seat? It makes your recent outing seem like you need a moment from some battle you fought out there. It makes coming home a relief.

As I make myself comfortable for the ride, I realize it's the same comfort your first cup of coffee brings in the morning, that blanketed welcome that allows your body to melt into your space. It aligns your mind for preparedness as the adventure begins.

I reach forward, turning the dial to play music. It's the only time I can sing my heart out. I found the true meaning of the lyrics in my car, ones I mindlessly had recited for so many years. Here is where I realized that I couldn't live without melody in my life. My discovery that there is a song for every moment and every occasion, how music can calm a disturbed soul, encourage positivity, and invigorate your senses. It is a rhythm that can play along with the mood of life.

The radio conversations and the daily news that you opt to listen to, because you can switch them off when it becomes unbearable. Podcasts, phone conversations, it's a thoughtless process we all take part in. Yet within this same space, I covered those endless conversations, deepest thoughts, tears of laughter, and how can I forget when the tears of another kind began to fall on some lengthy journey. I wiped them away and pulled myself together again right in this seat.

It's in my car, and I can adjust my body temperature perfectly. It shelters me from the elements, and when the breeze passes through the open windows, I feel free. I can align my thoughts here and venture into possible outcomes that seem attainable. It's this very seat that has molded my externalities and this very enclosure that sets me apart from the rest of the traffic. Even when I'm lost and the maps direct me, I feel safe right here in this seat. I've enjoyed some of the most breathtaking views in this moving vehicle. A ride has coaxed me into the deepest slumber, like a baby rocked to sleep as I got chauffeured home. And when the real babies appeared, I carried that precious cargo with so much attentiveness. It's this seat that reminded me that another life was more valuable than my own.

I glance at the rearview mirror, and I'm reminded that looking behind is essential even though going forward is important. I find it reassuring that reversing does take more effort than mindlessly driving ahead. Now and again, you should look back at what you left and see how far you have come and everything you have achieved. Just like parallel parking, we make ourselves fit in someplace, and if we don't, we move on until we find a place that allows for our space. The struggle is real, and eventually, we master the unattainable.

The side views instill some sense of space. We all share the roads. Even though the luxuries inside our box may be different, outside, we are no different. Each time someone passes me, I'm reminded of the race we run constantly to keep up. The road is the same; we all eventually go back to what brought us here. As I pass by, I'm aware yet surprised at our tendency to take things for granted, and we do it unknowingly. The lanes within which we travel do allow us to stay focused and alert. When our time comes, we will eventually drift off on our own.

It doesn't matter whether you own a luxury vehicle; the ride is the same. We maneuver from A to B and back again. What sets us apart is the distance we travel, how we use our time, and what we do with our imagination when isolation sets in.

Separation

It wasn't until I was separated from that world did I know the true meaning of heartache. Not only the ache you feel from people you lose, but the ache you feel deep down, being separated from the comfortable surroundings you once thrived in. I feel the heartache of being separated from a nation I was born into. I took a silent journey back to what I once called home.

I was sent away to be protected from the conflict that ignited between the two countries. Without a second thought, I traveled to a nearby nation and made home there, alone, to be sheltered. I probed their decisions about my life, and without a choice, I was ushered with a bag and a goodbye.

Every day, I questioned the morals of two nations, the justification of invasion. There is no road to victory once innocent lives are threatened, families and homes are torn apart, and lives are lost.

This train ride doesn't seem to end, and with no end in sight, my anxiety refuses to shed. An air ride would have taken less time, but no planes are landing where I'm headed. In my seclusion, every day, I longed to be in the arms of my mother and to be sitting next to my father. They tell me I left, so I don't understand what they live with every day. But did they understand the depth of my depressive state and how I managed without them, and how I struggled with a new beginning? I may not understand what it is like to live amidst destruction, but I survived in a traumatic state of distress every day. Worry and concern consumed every inch of my being. What is the point in advancing in technology when a war strips you of your ability to communicate? I waited tirelessly for phone calls and watched the media hype up every attack, and then I suffered with the troubled silence until I heard that one awaited voice on the other end telling me, "All is well." No, they don't understand. You don't gain relief, it's a never-ending cycle of agonizing torture, thinking the unknown.

I realized that when you leave something behind, it stays behind. I walk the same streets that are all too familiar but now seem foreign to me. My emotions switch within minutes as I glance at my friend's face. We laugh over coffee in the city where we finally reunite, and in one glance, silence draws a veil over me. My body shudders to see the hundreds of pictures that line the Great Wall, faces of people who lost their lives in this battle. What happened to my country, my people, and my home? People walk the streets as if nothing is wrong. I suppose normalcy sinks in amidst this turmoil. The tug between defeat and victory amongst nations equals the ideology that humanitarianism barely exists when power is at stake. It revolts me that I came back to a war scene.

I walk into my parents' home. There is an uneasy exhaustion that fills the space, a feeling of not belonging, and an unexplainable distance between us. Within a few years, everything changed, but her cooking, his hospitality, and the love haven't changed. They share their disconcertion, and I can only imagine. Picking themselves up at 2 a.m. to the sound of sirens and seeking shelter, hour after hour, huddled together with like-minded fear. The melancholy air refuses to leave as I sit and imagine how, when their eyes finally met the sunlight, they saw their world torn apart. No, I don't know what that was like. I don't know how you watch losing buildings to missiles and losing neighbors to unexpected death. I don't know what it feels like to watch soldiers pace the streets and weapons of destruction around every corner. How do you stumble over rubble and mourn remains? How do you grab your belongings and run for your life? I don't know how your home becomes a temporary cage. I don't even know how they let me go so they could suffer like this.

Tomorrow, I'll take the same 20-hour journey back to my home, because that is where I belong now. She fed me her best meals, the ones I craved. I received an embrace only a father can provide, as I saw in his eyes, the years of labor he tirelessly sweated for me. I let them be; they have each other. I can see clearly how a war couldn't separate their love, even when I pleaded for her to come with me. Why was it that fathers, sons, brothers, and husbands were held hostage and forbidden to leave, even when they disagreed with this war? All they wanted for me was a life, safe and secure beyond this disbelief. I understand now how I had to separate, to make them happy, even if that meant heartache for me and the country I once called home.

Cry If You Want To

When I watched his tears fall, the innocent drops fell without conviction. He wiped them quickly, for fear of not wanting to be seen in such a state. I embraced him as wholly as I could. I gave him my shoulder, and he resisted. I was puzzled. He's allowed to be vulnerable; this loss was his just as much as mine. I had sheltered him all his life, mending his every hurt. Now, when he's taller and stronger than I am, I just assumed he was able to deal with his emotions. I was wrong. My motherly instinct told me something was very wrong.

For a while, I forgot my pain because when your child is hurting, you lose your senses. I could see the same devastation in his face, the same sorrow, and the same tears I was experiencing. We hugged, and as I felt his overwhelming heart barely beat, I also felt the heaviness of the cry that needed to be released, but somehow was being forced in. Why was he resisting?

Why is it that we disregard the tears a man needs to cry. Why is it looked down upon when they show such vulnerability? He's human after all; he feels, he hurts. Why should he bottle up his emotions? I fail to believe women are the only emotional creatures. We are openly allowed to display our cries. Without a second thought, we are comforted and consoled. Yet a man has to hide and battle the cyclone of thoughts and eruption of emotions out of fear that he would become less of a man.

It was the first time since he had grown up that I felt his emotions more than mine. I never talked to him about opening up to his, and

I was guilty; as a young mother, I told him, "Boys don't cry." I never for one moment questioned the reasons behind my words. And now, when all he wanted to do was cry, I couldn't make him. He couldn't express the same rights that were given to me, even expected of me.

Society has led us to believe a man's strength lies in his dignity, but under that armor, he too holds a tender heart, one that feels and suffers emotional pain. Men, too, yearn for affection, but it's disregarded for them to solicit such behavior because it will tarnish their image. Being vulnerable doesn't discount your value as a man. It shows you, too, are human.

Yes, we're built differently. It's in our makeup not to want to display certain behaviors. Yes, we are wired differently, too, but our hearts pump equally, they hurt equally, and they break as well. Our tears were meant to be shed, and our hearts were meant to feel the ache. Suppressing their struggles only erupts in other forms of behavior; perhaps that is why silence and anger dominate their anatomy.

It's affection we all crave; to be understood. What is felt and how it is processed to what we present bears a disconnect for men. Somehow, being sensitive and crying makes them feel less of a man. We unknowingly burden them with our emotions and the need to be understood. In the same way, how do we allow these souls to walk amongst us as if they feel no pain or sadness, and releasing tears becomes a sign of weakness?

I held on to him until he could release those tears. I, too, felt a sense of relief. For some time, I forgot I was the one who needed to be held. We both lost someone that day, but we both formed a mindful bond. I looked up at those teary, misty brown eyes as I touched his supple cheek. "It's ok to cry. Boys can cry. You can cry if you need to."

My Neighbor Val

She smoked like a chimney. Back then, it was a common scene. Her croaky voice and stained teeth justified her obsession with cigarettes. Val was our next-door neighbor. She was in her mid-life, older than my parents. A slender, tall housewife to a husband who was of similar stature, yet so different. It was then that I figured out that opposites did attract. George didn't speak as much as Val, and we also didn't see him as much. He never smoked.

We'd meet mostly in the garden, cigarette in one hand and a cup of tea in the other, or she'd have the cigarette hanging from her mouth while she clipped her washing on the clothesline or straightened her plant pots. Her curly short hair blew slightly in the breeze. She wore high-waisted jeans and cozy slippers that she never took off, in rain or shine. A pack of cigarettes and a lighter were permanent fixtures in her hand. She'd always stop her chore to say, "Hello, luv," walking closer to the short wired fence that separated our gardens. Without a thought, she'd begin to mention the latest news about another neighbor or how the dustbin men left the gate open again to the entrance we shared. She'd voice her annoyance with the paper boy. He didn't throw her newspaper directly at her doorstep, and so it got half drenched in the rain.

Every conversation was eventually interrupted with a hacking cough filled with phlegm. Val talked with my dad at length. He would sometimes share drinks with her in the garden. My mother, on the other hand, would wave from a distance mainly because she was put off by the smoke that never left Val's side.

Val would invite me over to her house so I could retrieve our empty dishes; my parents would send over food they thought she'd enjoy. They loved sharing, and it didn't faze them that Val never once cooked for them. Her house had a stale stench, and there was not much color. Some parts of her living space seemed untouched. I felt sorry for the kettle that whistled nonstop, perched on her stove top. China teacups and saucers with used tea bags filled her sink. The oven light was always on, along with her television that was situated in front of a worn armchair. I knew it was her chair because there was an ashtray right next to it. The house wasn't as orderly as I thought it should be, considering she was home all the time. Cereal boxes and newspapers lined her kitchen workspace. I couldn't imagine Val cooking a meal. The bread bin was always open, overflowing with packets of half-used loaves. On top of the bin was her stock of cigarette packets, stacked like the Leaning Tower of Pisa. There was always a newspaper resting on her chair, one on the foot, and one beside the ashtray. I often wondered if perhaps there was more to her than met the eye. She was a walking encyclopedia of current affairs.

I didn't know much else about Val. I didn't even know her full name. The couple replicated somewhat of a TV sitcom. A mundane life, repetitive events, and once in a while, the need to gossip about the surrounding neighbors. Val and George never argued, and I thought that odd, too. She had only one daughter who lived so far away she barely saw her. I wondered what she did in her spare time, as it seemed like she had an abundance of it. She never left the house. George did all the shopping and chores; he also went to work. I never saw any friends or visitors come and go. Our home, on the other hand, was like a zoo on Saturday mornings in comparison.

Val noticed every visitor, and she'd question me afterwards about raised voices and arguments she overheard on the street.

Every Christmas, Val would give me underwear. It seemed embarrassing but amusing. I realize now, it was quite thoughtful. Girls need pretty underwear. Val always remembered my birthday, and secretly, I'd wait for her to knock on the door when I got home from school. Val would hand over an envelope in exchange for some birthday cake. It was that little bit of excitement that she gave me that made her a special neighbor. She often mentioned what a good girl I was to my parents. She always noticed my new haircut or my new coat. She made me feel special amongst my siblings.

Her simplicity is what inspired me the most; her ability to be content with herself, with so little. Yes, Val smoked non-stop, drank a lot of tea, read boring newspapers, and watched TV all day long on her worn armchair because it made her happy. It didn't seem to bother her that George didn't have his chair or that he did her chores. Every day she stood by her bay window, sipping a cup of tea and watching the world go by through the sheer net curtains. I'd look up to see if she was standing there on my way home from school, and Val would wave back. She lived in her world and did whatever pleased her.

Years later, I ventured back to spy on my neighbor Val. Our full house was empty, somewhat torn apart. No more parents, scattered siblings, no chaos, but the house stood sturdy. Val's house stood solid next to it. Val was still there. She had aged quite a bit; her wrinkles were deeper, her hair like silver coils, and her voice croaked more than ever. Her need to grasp a moment for air in between her sentences disturbed me. This time, I had a cup of tea with her, and my heart sank as she reminisced about the days gone by. She told me she missed me, the little girl next door, with a big smile. George had passed; she had outlived my younger parents. Val was still going strong, living her simple, content life, watching the world go by.

Soul Sister

It was like hugging a piece of my past. A past I almost forgot existed. The fact that I was standing in the middle of the rush in the arrivals lane of the busy airport didn't faze me one bit. Everything would wait, the noise, the cars, the people, I blanked it all away as I held on to nostalgia.

We grew up together, in different households, but the same family. We walked through life together, sometimes not seeing each other for years, but our lives always ran parallel. Today, after decades, I was about to get some closure. I was going to acquire the motherly comfort, the sisterly love, and the best friend bond that only a person who lived without can understand. I like to think I single-handedly manifested this meet, but I know full well that it takes two people to build on a relationship of this magnitude.

She's not just another family member; she's not even just another person. She's my soul sister. My connection to so much of my turbulent history. She is my dictionary for words that don't exist within the boundaries of my life. It's a past like ours that makes you bitter and withdrawn.

For us, though, we had that one antidote that kept us intact: We had each other. We always managed to laugh it away. Even in the painful moments, we covered them nicely for each other. We laughed away pain so the other could understand when no one else could. Laughter does so much more than just make you happy in the moment. It eliminated our need to be somber. We didn't see a reason to stop. We laughed because we wore it the best of all the possible choices; we looked our best when we laughed it away.

Today, I will celebrate the meeting of survival, I will celebrate an everlasting bond. When I look forward, I see us still holding on to each other; it's rare what we have. Looking back makes it unreal. Lost parents, damaged relationships, marriage, distance, and life threw us off course. Somehow, we always steered back to that inseparable connection we held. It's real. Superficial doesn't exist in our world.

We're stronger now, walking more confidently as we're aging gracefully. I straighten her crown as she wipes my tears, and together we hold on to a little bit of the past that needed nurturing just a tad more. I know, in another week when I come back to this very place that makes goodbyes hard, these very tears of happiness will turn to tears of the saddest farewell, and I will stand here and hold on to nostalgia once again.

As I released from the embrace, reality sank in. The noise of my surroundings filled my ears again. I glanced at her face, which matured like our relationship. The smile hasn't changed, like the person who never gave up on me.

Welcome to My Home

It's a reflection of me. It's what sets the stage for my persona. Everyone's home tells a story. I learn a lot about people when I enter their homes. I see what is important to them. What I read in their space sums up chapters of the person I visit.

Every visitor who comes through my door needs to feel welcome and also learn a little about me through my dwelling. My home is not a masquerade, rather a piece of my land where I do as I please, so the authentic vibes cradle all who are welcomed in.

No matter where I am in the world, after some time, I'll begin to miss my safe haven. It's my happy place, where I can be myself, and I can let go and function on my timetable. It's the space that protects me from the exterior clatter of the world, from the elements and the unnecessary noise. The comfort a home brings elevates its beauty. It should manifest a positive atmosphere and disperse the same to all who enter. Where you spend the most important time is your home, where you switch off from the world, and the place you awaken to a new beginning is your home.

I'm an orderly person, and so things are always in their place. One-of-a-kind pieces fill my den. If zen were a color, it would be green. Numerous plants fill my empty spaces, and it helps draw the outdoors inside. I proudly display the majestic pieces of my origins; each item displayed in my home holds a story, and each piece has a special meaning. The artifacts in my home hold a bond; they tell a tale. My walls house art: I picked them out because they speak to me. Earthy tones dashed with a splash of color here and there invite togetherness. Books bind my space and candles light my evenings. The smell of incense unites my youth to the present day, and the abundance of frames helps me remember loved ones. The constant sound of music rejuvenates my soul. Above all, the picturesque view from my windows ties my little home together with the big, wide world. My home speaks volumes; it tells a story to all who enter my doors.

Your home is where you uncover your true being, where the bare feet and the organic body dwell. Your home is where you speak your mind and shed tears in silence. It's where you wash off the worries of the day and where you lay your head for slumber. It's where you pray for forgiveness. Your most imperative decisions are made within those four walls. Your home is where the real you comes alive and where you transform yourself for the world that awaits outside. And each time I step outside the door, I remember, there is only one key that is of importance. The key to my home is where my heart resides.

The Strays

I'm all coffeed out, so I wait for a friend to grab one. I sit at the window and watch the passersby. My eyes fixate on a stray dog, which lies peacefully on the dusty path, and the pedestrians dodge by as if it's an ornamented part of the pavement. My heart melts as I examine his stature. I'm not sure what breed he is. His innocent face is nestled in his chest. His eyes are closed, and his camel-colored coat shows off the dust from the Delhi roads. He needs grooming, and I try to picture him that way. What a beautiful animal he would be. His cute puppy face reminds me of my two precious dogs, and I feel sorry that these helpless ones have to sleep on the streets when they should be loved in a home.

A street cleaner wakes him from his slumber by nudging him with a broom made up of branches. It must be his duty to keep the shopping center free from debris, although you couldn't tell that his job was done all that well. The animal does as he is told. He gets up slowly, almost as if he's used to the annoying interference. He walks a few steps; I see him limping, and I feel even worse. He doesn't seem as malnourished as some I have come across, and it eases my concern a little. A nearby couple shoo him away, and he looks sadder than perhaps he is.

How do dogs become stray here? Do owners just abandon them? They don't seem to be harmed in any way. I suppose people just leave them to it. It's heartbreaking. Just like beggars, they too roam the streets in search of the basics to survive.

Another fellow animal lover pats him lovingly and instantly, and I feel better knowing some of us who feel for these creatures, the ones who can't speak for themselves. I ask my friend if I can feed it, and I'm instantly scolded as if I spoke the forbidden words. "They're stray and can be wild, you never know," I'm told. Yes, but whose fault is that really, and aren't we partially responsible for that? It's not their fault.

We step out of the coffee shop, and I make eye contact with the dog. I tried, I tell it. His sweet puppy eyes glisten in the dusk, and my heart skips a beat. I take a mental picture so I can remember him. I'm grateful that people just leave them alone. As I walk away, I turn around to check on him. If I could, I would take you home.

Agree to Disagree

I stood in the great room and tried so hard to see what my friend saw. The colors morphed into one big mess, and I failed to recognize the story she painted for me. Over and over again she explained it, and I was as perplexed as the moment I first laid my eyes on it. Nothing was making sense, and even though I read the small description, my curiosity only expanded.

The ginormous masterpiece hung by itself, isolated from the rest of the museum pieces. Perhaps that is the reason; it's a complicated, mysterious work of art. It had to be given a room of its own so you could connect with it, distinguish and study it, and therefore it could be understood.

She left my side eventually and wandered off, giving up on me because I wouldn't give up on this, which became a challenge. I stood there like a child in front of a blackboard trying to solve a math equation. Spectators came and left satisfied, whispering and agreeing amongst themselves. I could have departed, too, but something kept me there. I stepped back, then left, then right, but nothing made sense. Feeling determined to connect the words with the brush strokes, I took deep sighs and allowed my eyes to detect every smear of the illustration.

Outcomes are all in how we perceive them. We can look at the same picture, but we will all see it differently. Our outlook is measured by our thoughts, and every thought has a purpose; isn't that how life works, too? Our perspective on how we want to see the picture changes everything. The tiniest of things can change your perception, like raindrops, for instance. Have you ever just stopped and watched them? Rain and tears have so much in common. They appear when times are gray or sad, but have you also noticed they both glisten and sparkle on a pretty petal or a delicate cheek?

As I've matured, I realized that it's okay to have an opinion, and it's also ok for others to have theirs. We don't have to agree. We can disagree amicably. What's not ok is to impose your beliefs on others. Whatever those may be. People lack the ability to listen, comprehend, and be satisfied with an undesirable outcome. If we only slowed down, and thought before we spoke, or let the situation sink in, before allowing ourselves to instantly mask in bitterness. We would not only perceive from a different angle, but we could also understand and be understood.

Tomorrow, will it matter? Will it have relevance weeks, months, or even years from now? Will you be willing to walk in my shoes? What if I left this world? Will that thought still hurt your ego? Will my opinion destroy your ability to live a fulfilling life? Everyone is entitled to an opinion, and if I disagree, it's not because I'm belittling your view; it's because I'm trying to understand why your view matters. I also want you to understand where I stand and why I see this view differently.

At times, I began envisioning the sad state in which my father left this world. No matter what I tried to entice him with on his deathbed, he didn't wake up. Nothing mattered, and so I began to realize we need life itself for anything to matter. The good, the bad, everything that takes up space in our minds, it's only validated because we are alive. Because we are alive, we have the opportunity to learn, explore, and equip ourselves with the ability to understand and be understood.

I left the painting for a while. Took a different approach entirely. When I revisited, I took a step back, and I did a retake of the entire story again. I couldn't wait to find my friend and tell her what I saw. It is possible. You can appreciate the view, permit change, see the picture a little differently, respond a little favorably, and allow yourself to coexist. Not because they're wrong, but you weren't either.

The Gentlemen's Club

There was a tinge of smokiness in the air, but not at all how I expected a cigar lounge to present itself. The low lights, relaxed atmosphere, and small crowds scattered here and there made this lounge inviting. Nevertheless, the outdoor seating enticed me more as I ordered my drink.

I stumbled upon this evening by chance, and here I was having meaningful conversations with three respectable middle-aged professional gentlemen. It didn't start that way; I was interrogated, as if it were a crime to show up and then be classy and well-spoken.

Once the liquid courage hit the parts of my brain that needed unchaining, I took the blows with ease. I felt I was being studied like a complicated textbook; you don't understand it, but you try your best to figure it out. I was judged. I should be used to it by now. I won't lie, at times I got agitated to the point of taking my leave.

To the left of me was a luxury car salesman. He was dressed as if he came from the showroom, quite robust, and straightforward, with much to say. He was opinionated and the initiator of the interrogation. To the right of me was a subdued medical professional, very easy-going and down-to-earth. He chose to listen mostly, paying a lot of attention to the interrogation and occasionally adding to it. Opposite me was my friend, the host for the evening. He's a VP, although you wouldn't have guessed it. He made himself very comfortable in front of me in his relaxed attire, as if he paid extra for prime seating. His intimidating demeanor portrays confidence, yet he gives off a very chill vibe, like nothing fazes him. I thought he'd be on my side, but he joined his buddies on the other side of the ring, very much amused. For sure, I'd get a report card from him tomorrow!

So, as I traveled this road of being tested as the only female made to feel like she needs to be accepted in this gentlemen's club, I thought to master my way for a comeback. I played with the ice cube in my glass. If I couldn't be the smooth, intense bourbon in my old-fashioned cocktail, I definitely wasn't going to be the cherries, no matter how sweet they were. I chose to be the solid piece of ice that took up the majority of space in my drink. After what seemed like the questions being hurled at me were exhausted, I demanded to ask just one question to all three: "What makes you worth knowing?"

Mr. VP decided to go first. His answer was fair; he has many friends from all walks of life, and so he networks and brings people together. In turn, they can help each other. Mr. Medical let Mr. Sales go next. I noticed he was struggling to get his answer together. Mr. Sales fumbled about how he also knows a lot of people, and he was great at what he does, and then piggybacked off of Mr. VP. Alas, came Mr. Medical, who cut it short, saying he would help anyone any way he could, but then added he would want the favor returned.

It amused me to see them amuse themselves. They discussed how tough this simple question was to answer. Not one of them asked me how unimpressed I was with their answers. They convinced themselves their answers were pretty good, yet a sense of insurability filled the air, clashing with the smoke.

I really was disappointed. Three grown professionals were put on the spot, and not one of them convinced me why they were worth knowing. I rested my case and took my leave, placing my drink down as the block of ice clashed with the glass. Now, the way to consume this cocktail is to savor the bourbon, devour the cherries, but you make sure that block of ice remains solid.

This experience assured me that showing up and standing my ground made me equal; I was just as smart and respectable as all three gentlemen, if not more. But being classy and well-spoken took me over the edge. I did get a report card the next day, just like I knew I would. I did pretty well. The report told me exactly why I was worth knowing and how that block of ice did anything but melt.

My Cutting-Edge Phone

We might as well have been born with them: smartphones. A bonus when you leave the hospital together with your birth certificate and car seat, you should get a phone assigned at birth. Smartphones have become as important as immediate necessities to survive these days. They're attached to us like an umbilical cord; the other end is a signal that represents the "lifeline." It was a lack of knowledge and technology that kept us generations apart, but now every generation has one thing in common: They all know how to operate a smartphone. I can't quite remember when they became so imperative in our lives, but now it's the one thing you can't leave home without.

Back in the day, we spoke via phone only when it was important. Cost played a huge part in our ability to have mindless conversations. Patience was a virtue, and it is missed. We waited to talk in person, observing body language, and engaging in interaction. I remember it being a luxury to have a mobile phone; now, one looks down on you if you don't have the newest model. The entire planet shifted to "keeping up with the latest and greatest." Trust me when I say the entire world is involved in this psychotic behavior. I have traveled to countries where being homeless is accepted, but being phoneless is not.

Instant information is at the top of the list today. With these devices, we have everything we need, and it's almost done without another human being involved. Our lives depend on our phones; they're our ticket to knowledge, instant communication, and connection to the world and beyond. Yet we survived without the gadget in the past; we made it through not knowing a great deal. Sometimes, too much knowledge is harmful. We're advancing into the digital world of Artificial Intelligence. It's called "artificial" for a reason. But as a human race, I believe we have taken many steps backwards. The more we advance in technology, we fall behind in primitive ideals: common sense, reasoning, native intelligence, and being real and present.

My longtime executive job consisted of using a phone daily, sometimes handling several lines at a time. I remember coming home and not wanting to answer the phone when it rang. It irritated me to talk after a long day hunched over a receiver. Today, we converse via a phone all day, even with those we see daily. It's become our storage bank. I remembered hundreds of numbers in my head. Now I barely remember any phone numbers. The overload of unwanted knowledge has taken up so much space.

Table manners now include phone etiquette. Phone distraction is a source of rudeness on so many levels. Our ability to simply wait has diminished, and with it the ability to obtain undivided attention. Unexpected death meant rummaging through personal belongings or diaries that would reveal secrets. Now everything is left on social media or in phones, together with secrets and hidden agendas for the world to find. There is no real privacy or seclusion. We were ok getting lost without a map and not making it home in time, and when you went missing for an hour or two, no one tracked you. Patience was really a virtue; now this phrase has no meaning. We require instant results. Waiting now is a cause of feud.

I must admit my phone did bring some positivity to my life. Being alone during the pandemic, it became that one lifeline that kept me afloat. It was my only source of reaching out for human interaction. It was my ticket to a little hope. I was never a person who used my phone immensely. But isolation caused me to become dependent on it. I feared losing it and began guarding it like a pet. Unknowingly, I let it dictate my existence. My phone was my door to the outside world I was isolated from. I walked around with it in my pocket, not wanting to miss any signal or response. It helped me through the toughest phase of my loneliness. It allowed me to have endless conversations with loved ones across the world. I could be a part of their life through social media, and when times got really tough, I had an avenue of support right at my fingertips. I couldn't see anyone in person, but video calls fulfilled that void too. I found myself documenting my journey through this phone, my writing, my photos; they all found a place right in my hand. My phone became my holy grail.

So, for whatever it's worth, technology and advancements do aid, sometimes in ways that are forbidden to acknowledge, because until we need help, we can't see that there is, in fact, a problem. For every problem we have recognized, there is always a solution. Cutting-edge advancements have led us into developments that are shaping our world for the better. Although some of us would like to go back to the way things were, it's really not all so bad to be part of the change; change is how we evolve, and change is good.

Take a Ride with Me

My small obsession with cars started young, when girls my age were into boys and makeup. I drooled over a metallic baby-blue Jaguar that glided past my house every morning. I'm not quite sure what drew me to slobber over such machinery, but I remember it being quite an attraction. I really think my liking of "classy" things began the moment I spotted this luxury automobile. It was a rare sight in my neighborhood. Not every household owned a vehicle, and most cars were second-hand, disfigured tin boxes that did nothing to please the eye.

It didn't take me long to figure out the Jaguar belonged to one of my bosses. I was hired for a part-time summer job. I would take a ten-minute walk to work. I found myself leaving the house at the exact time every day, so I could drool over this beauty passing by. Then one day, as it poured down with rain and I struggled with my umbrella against the unforgiving wind, this four-wheeled stunner halted at my side. The passenger window glided down, and a well-groomed gentleman of a boss signaled for me to take the back seat. I remember him mumbling something about how I'd never make it on time to clock in as I fumbled with my belongings. I was so stunned; I almost wanted to throw the umbrella away so I could focus on getting into the car.

It was that exact moment I had experienced, for the first time, the "new car" scent. Every moment after that, when I have seated myself in a brand-new car, I go back in time to the very moment I entered this vehicle. I don't recall the rest of the conversation between my boss and me. I just recall what I felt.

I came from a mediocre upbringing. My father's idea of a luxury car was the eyesore of a station wagon parked outside our house. He worked on the Renault all the time; in fact, I don't remember any car he owned that didn't need work. Tirelessly, he'd change spark plugs, timing belts, and gearboxes. He would fiddle with the cassette player and speakers. I'd sit in the passenger seat with a pencil and wind back the cassette tapes that got caught in the player. I would help him with tools, hold flashlights, and wash the car.

Sitting in this Jaguar was like getting to experience a little bit of heaven. The creamy leather felt so rich, as if I were seated on a lush cloud. I almost wasn't aware we had started driving off; the silence inside was undisturbed, and no street noise made its way in. The floor mats were spotless, and the clear windows sold the raindrops to me. The windshield wipers glided effortlessly, syncing with the sound of the symphony playing in the background, and became hypnotizing. The wooden steering wheel made it look as though it was effortless to maneuver this vessel. The same varnished wood was embellished inside the door frames and along the dashboard. I never knew a car could make me feel so majestic, and here I was breathing in the very essence of being driven in the back of a Jaguar.

It was the same uneven, bumpy road I traveled in my dad's car, and yet here, it seemed like I was sailing smoothly across water. I didn't want to exit this luxury compartment; it made me feel like the world beyond this vehicle was anything but safe. The majestic Jaguar cat emblem that protruded from the bonnet of the car made me feel royal. I'll always remember the sleek lines across the polished body and the masterpiece of a glossy interior. It was then that I found wheels and rims aesthetically pleasing.

It was this beauty that made me want to learn to drive. It was this experience that allowed me to educate myself on engines, horsepower, transmissions, engaging dashboards, and appealing exteriors. Over the years, I have been blessed to be able to drive many-sized vehicles, from SUVs to sports cars. I have some favorites, but the Jaguar XJ was once a symbol of British motoring excellence. It was my first luxury car experience, and it will always be my first love.

You Crossed My Path

I find myself at sea, sailing the waters, and for every wave that creates turbulence, I must hang tight. The smooth sailing is abruptly forgotten when the storms arrive, and I hold on for my life. Each storm taught me a different lesson, and by now I know every inch of this vessel. Yet as I sail happily with the wind blowing through my hair, an unexpected soul lost at shore needs rescuing, and I am present once again. I forget my life is just as important. I forget I have to save myself, too. I give and rarely take, and that is how my ship begins to sink.

You crossed my path, and I hesitated, and then, with time, I let you stay. When you left, that's when I learned the lesson. For every person that has crossed my path, I eventually thanked each and every one for the conversations, experiences, and for the scriptures they left upon my soul. I believe now everything happens for a reason, and every person who touches my life does so for a reason. There are lessons we all must learn, and until we learn those lessons, we will continue to be handed assignments until one day we pass the test. Until one day we figure out how to sail forward, to not look back, to forgive, and no longer regret. Now, a stronger version of me emerges and sets sail once again.

Life lessons cannot be taught, and there is no manual on this ship. I began to put up a guard and set my own boundaries. I learn your flaws first so I may use them against you, and that way, I can navigate this pull and, in turn, hurt less when you decide I no longer deserve to be in your life. I have no desire to conquer the waters if victory means I must dampen another soul. You see, if you held my hand with even an inch of love, then blemishing you is impossible for me. My conscience doesn't allow me to hurt the one I once embraced; I'd let you go silently, lovingly. You don't get to choose the way I feel, or if I feel. You get to choose if you stay; you get to choose if I am worthy of your love. I am steering this secure soul, I choose whom I love deeply, and I am also aware that eventually I will hurt just as much.

Then the universe presented me with another earthly episode, one in which no matter how hard I try, what is to happen will happen. It's called destiny. Destiny speaks a language of its own, one that the wise understand. You cannot change the manner in which your life unfolds; you can think all you want. What has happened and what is happening are irrelevant to what we don't know about tomorrow.

I mended my unbalanced vessel once you left. I began another journey through different waters. The essence of my vitality showed me, for every night there is a morning waiting, for every tear there is a smile illuminating, and for every goodbye there is another welcome. I was worthy of every embrace I took, and I am worthy of every breath I inhale, and every anchor I released allowed me to come up and rejuvenate my unbalanced soul. For every chance I took, a new version of me emerged. The direction in which I maneuver my sails is my prerogative.

You left me a gift of a hurtful wound, and the sea breeze helped me turn it into a scar that will remind me I survived our journey. I'm navigating these waters with some resilience, faith, and a little panache because you happened to cross my path, and you will never know the mark you left upon my soul and the lessons you taught my heart.

About the Author

Meet Sunita

Originally from England, Sunita settled in the US, where she co-founded and built a successful enterprise based in the Washington, DC, area. She raised her two boys and then left the corporate world to focus on her true purpose in life. She became a mentor, teacher, and life coach. Her solo journey through midlife in Miami allowed her to reflect on everyday experiences; Sunita discovered herself through her writing. Those who know her best would say she's the kind of person who cares deeply, listens intensely, laughs easily, and finds inspiration in the little moments that make life meaningful — qualities that shine through in every story she tells; resulting in the birth of this book.

www.sunitasspace.com

Photography by Shirah Stern

www.ingramcontent.com/pod-product-compliance
Lightning Source LLC
Chambersburg PA
CBHW061122100726
47911CB00013B/640
9798993848204